Seduction

CLAW & WARDER

Episode 1

ERIK HENRY VICK

RATATOSKR PUBLISHING

NEW YORK

RATATOSKR PUBLISHING
2080 NINE MILE POINT ROAD, UNIT 106
PENFIELD, NY 14526

PUBLISHER'S NOTE: THIS IS A WORK OF FICTION. NAMES, CHARACTERS, PLACES, AND INCIDENTS ARE A PRODUCT OF THE AUTHOR'S IMAGINATION. LOCALES AND PUBLIC NAMES ARE SOMETIMES USED FOR ATMOSPHERIC PURPOSES. ANY RESEMBLANCE TO ACTUAL PEOPLE, LIVING OR DEAD, OR TO BUSINESSES, COMPANIES, EVENTS, INSTITUTIONS, OR LOCALES IS COMPLETELY COINCIDENTAL.

SEDUCTION/ ERIK HENRY VICK. -- 1ST ED.
ISBN 978-1-951509-03-3

TABLE OF CONTENTS

In memory of Jerry Orbach, one of the greatest.

Special thanks to Stephen Jacobs who helped me with all things Jewish. If there are any errors, they are mine and not his.

I'm sorry your help resulted in a *herem* for you, Steve!

I hope you enjoy *Seduction*. If so, please consider joining my Readers Group—details can be found at the end of the last chapter.

CHAPTER I

THE BODY

In the Locus of New York, crimes committed by magical entities threaten the delicate balance between the mundane world and the supernatural realm.

The dedicated teams of detectives who investigate these breaches of Canon and Covenants are members of an elite unit known as the Supernatural Inquisitors Squad.

These are their stories.

I

Two women stepped into Riverside Park from the corner of West 106th Street and Riverside Drive. They were dressed in "running gear," though neither had any intention of moving at anything faster than a stroll. Lifelong friends, their pace seemed set by mutual, though unspoken, accord.

Kylelynn Fubelli lifted her eyes toward the sky and sighed. The temperature lingered at just above chilly, and threatening, ugly gray clouds loomed over them. "Will spring ever come?" she muttered.

Amie Brewer chuckled and patted her friend's shoulder. "Yes, but until then, keep your eyes off the gloom and on the hot chunks of man-flesh who jog in this park. That should be enough to keep you warm."

Kylelynn laughed, rolling her eyes. "What about Dave?"

"Dave's not here, man," said Amie in her best Tommy Chong voice.

"Has anyone tried to have you committed this week?"

"Dave-schmave. What he doesn't know won't kill him." Amie peered up at Kylelynn's face. "Besides, you're married, not dead."

"'Look, but never touch," Kylelynn said and laughed.

"I swear to God, Ky, you are such a little Girl Scout. Maybe you can touch one? A little bit, anyway, and only in the right places."

"Oh, you're bad!" Even so, Kylelynn's eyes danced with an excitement she tried to deny—or at least keep hidden.

"Bad? Me?" Amie flashed a mischievous smile, then lifted her chin to point down the path ahead of them. "Like him. Check out that posterior!" She chuckled as she said it.

Kylelynn said nothing. In fact, she'd stopped ten paces behind Amie and was staring into the underbrush. "Oh my God!" she croaked.

"What is it?" asked Amie. "It can't be better than that hunk up ahead."

"Do you have your phone?" The color drained from Kylelynn's face, and she drew rapid, shallow breaths.

Amie glanced at the brush at the side of the path but made no move to return to her friend's side. "What is it?" she asked again.

"We don't want to get involved with anyone off the paths, Kylelynn. You know that."

"Give me your phone." It came out in a breathless rush, almost a whisper.

"Come on, hon," said Amie. "Whatever it is, let's leave it."

"Your phone!"

Amie heaved a sigh and trudged back toward Kylelynn. "Come on, Ky. We don't want to ruin the morning. Not over a homeless..." She stopped talking as she caught a glimpse of what had captured Kylelynn's attention. "Sweet Jesus, Mother Mary, and Blessed Joseph," Amie murmured. She swung her pack off her shoulder and fished for her cell phone, never once allowing her gaze to leave the dried-out husk hidden in the underbrush.

2

Leery Oriscoe heaved a sigh as he pulled himself out of the car and into the brisk, overcast morning. He wore a camel hair overcoat buttoned to the neck with a scarf tucked carefully under his chin. His brownish-gray hair rustled in the breeze, and he smoothed it with an irritated glance at the sky. He considered getting the black hat out of the trunk, but that belonged to his darker half and signified a belief that Leery no longer shared.

He lifted his face slightly and sniffed the air—as if his sense of smell was as refined as a tracking dog's. He wrinkled his nose and sneezed.

"Catching a cold, Detective?" asked a uniformed officer as he approached from the park.

"Something like that," said Leery. "You the one who called me?"

"Jim Butcher," the cop said.

Leery nodded in an absent-minded way. "You're from the Two Seven, right? I recognize you."

"Sure," said Butcher.

"Right." Leery sighed and shook his head. "Better take me to it, Jim."

"Sure thing, Detective." The uniformed policeman turned his back on the street and strode into the park.

With another sigh, Leery followed. "Anyone else from the house here yet?"

Butcher shook his head. "No dicks. Just cops," he said.

"Hey, detectives are cops, Butcher."

Butcher lifted his hand and waved it. "Sure thing. Whatever you say, Oriscoe."

"Answer me this, Butcher. Why us? Why call in the Special Investigations Squad? Your regular detectives will want to skin you alive."

Again, Butcher lifted his hand and waved it. "Sure, sure. You'll see in a second."

"Oh, a mystery! I just *love* mysteries." Leery rolled his eyes.

Butcher led him to a section of the path that had been blocked off with yellow crime scene tape. Two women in running suits stood off to the side, their heads together.

"So, Jim... Are those my two witnesses colluding over there?"

Butcher glanced over his shoulder. "Colluding?"

Leery drew a deep breath and let it out in a rush. "Where I come from, Officer Butcher, we keep the wits separated until we can take their statement. You know, we try to discourage them 'getting their stories straight.'"

Butcher stopped and waved his hand toward the two women. "Well, there they are, *Detective*. Feel free to tell them to stop talking."

Leery cocked his head and looked down his impressive nose at the cop. "Better show me the body first, Butcher."

"Sure thing."

"And I gotta say, Butcher, your attitude leaves a little room for improvement this morning."

As Leery stepped into the brush, he glanced back toward the street. A stunning blonde turned into the park and walked toward him, her gaze locked on his own. "Sweet God," Leery muttered.

Butcher turned to look and let out a low whistle. "Key-rist! What a knockout."

"She one of your detectives?"

Butcher shook his head. "I'd remember a piece like that."

Leery glanced at him with a wry expression. "*All* those sensitivity classes were money well-spent, I see."

Without taking his eyes off the blonde, Butcher hawked and spat into the woods.

The blonde came on, her gaze boring into Leery's as if no one else existed. "She's either a cop, or it's my lucky day." He scoffed. "My lucky century."

Sparing a single glance at the two witnesses, the blonde woman walked right up to Leery and stuck out her hand. "Oriscoe?" she asked.

"That's me," said Leery, taking her small hand in his scarred paw. "Tell me you're not a process server."

"Okay. I'm not a process server." She glanced at Butcher, then returned her gaze to Leery's face. As their eyes met, her features shifted, blurring a little around the edges. Her hair darkened and darkened until it was a shade of black so impervious to color that it reflected the ambient light as blue highlights. Her once-blue eyes also darkened, settling on a deep red. A set of black horns sprouted from high on her forehead and pushed skyward. Even her clothing shifted from a light and airy spring dress to a black leather pants and jacket combo. A staff capped with a blood garnet leaned in the crook of her shoulder. "I'm your new partner, Detective Nogan. Call me Dru."

"I thought you'd be a man." His darker half squirmed within him, hackles rising.

"Disappointed?" she asked.

"Hey, I'm old, not dead." He never once dropped his gaze away from hers. She wasn't the first succubus he'd met.

3

While Butcher looked on, Leery stood there like an idiot, staring at the woman—at the succubus—who was to be his new partner. Detectives in the Supernatural Inquisitors Squad always went in pairs, but Leery's last partner had...moved on. Leery was what they called a Claw—his dark half would provide the muscle in the partnership—and that meant Dru was his Warder. She would use her skill at wizardry to protect his back—and in her unique case, her magical charms.

The mundane cops knew nothing about their squad or its practices—nothing beyond the image cultivated by the powers that ran everything in the Locus of New York—they didn't even know the squad's real name. They all thought the "Special Investigations Squad" was made up of elite, veteran detectives who took all the weird, unsolvable homicide cases and solved them.

The only problem was that Dru looked about seventeen, and the image she'd presented earlier—the bombshell blonde—looked about as much like a detective as Leery did a male underwear model. Leery glanced at Butcher and found him squinting at Dru's face, his gaze taking little detours to check out the rest of her body every few seconds.

"I've heard a lot about you, Oriscoe," said Dru, narrowing her eyes. "I want you to know I'm coming at this with an open mind. I'm not here to judge."

Leery flashed his special smile at her—the one he used to make skells piss their pants. The one that was all teeth and dark promises. "I'll try not to hold it against you, either."

"What?" asked Dru.

"You know," he said, waving his hand at her body. "Just don't turn it at me."

Dru lifted her chin and let it slowly fall back to its normal position. "Yeah."

"Dicks," muttered Butcher, shaking his head. "Look, you want to see the body, or you want to stand here talking in riddles?"

Leery tilted his head to the side, a half-grin on his lips. "Butcher's in a rush this morning. He's got an appointment to have the stick removed from his—"

"Yes," said Dru, her gaze shifting to Butcher. "Please, Officer Butcher. Take us to it."

Leery wrinkled the skin on his nose and followed the other two into the brush. He had a few more jibes saved up for cops like Butcher, but they'd have to wait.

The body—if you could call what was left of the man a body—was fifteen paces beyond the edge of the asphalt path. The remains looked desiccated, sucked dry. The skin had turned gray and shriveled—more like remains mummified by heat and exposure than a fresh body.

"The medical examiner is sending someone over," said Butcher. He looked down at the body for a moment. "What could do that to a body? I mean, New York ain't exactly a desert."

"Chemicals," said Leery, his gaze locked on Dru's.

"Sure," she said. "Industrial cleaners and the like."

"Go call the medical examiner, Butcher," said Leery. "We won't be needing them."

"What? Procedure says—"

"We'll use our own people. It's in our purview to decide whether to keep it all in-house or not, and this time, we'll handle it all ourselves."

Butcher lifted an eyebrow and stared at Leery. "If you say so."

"I do." Leery tipped him a wink and flashed a patronizing smile.

With a shrug, Butcher turned back toward the path. "Sure thing. Whatever you want."

Dru pulled her phone out of somewhere— her skintight leather outfit didn't come with pockets, and she didn't seem to carry a purse—and dialed the Office of the Magical Examiner. Like The Supernatural Inquisition Squad, the Magical Examiner's Office existed within the same system as their mundane counterparts as a special unit.

"You know what this looks like," said Leery. He tried to make it sound casual, but his voice was rough, harsh.

She looked at him as she spoke to the ME. Her expression betrayed nothing.

"Because to me, it looks like our friend here ran into a—"

"Yes!" she snapped. "I know how it looks."

"Didn't mean to step on your toes," said Leery.

"I'm only half-succubus," said Dru in a stage-whisper.

"That blonde thing is quite a trick, though."

"Can't help that," she said. "It's how you and Butcher wanted me to look."

"What? I didn't—"

"It's a subconscious drive, Oriscoe. Relax."

Leery turned back to the husk and waved at it. "Am I wrong? Looks like—"

"The last remains of a meal for one of my mother's kind. You aren't wrong."

Leery peeked at her askance. "And it won't be a problem?"

She threw back her head and laughed. "If you only knew... My mother and I haven't spoken in decades, Oriscoe."

"Your mother's a..."

"The word is 'succubus,' Detective, and yes. I couldn't be part succubus unless my mother was one."

"I suppose if your father was an incubus you'd—"

"I'd be male."

"Oh, is that how it works?"

"It is," she said with an air of finality. "Now, you've had your bit of fun. Can we get to work?"

"Trust me, Nogan. This isn't my idea of fun."

"Right. Help me roll him."

"Don't you want to wait for the Magical Examiner?"

Dru shook her head. "The CSI guys will be able to reconstruct anything we disturb."

Leery suppressed a shudder. "I suppose you're right. I hate those guys."

Dru shrugged. "They're just like us."

Leery scoffed. "Hardly. I don't commune with the spirit world to do my job."

"That's because you can't. If you could, you'd be working for them."

"Yeah, sure," said Leery. He squatted near the body's head. "Let's roll him, then."

Dru grabbed the man's feet, and they rolled him face up.

"Jumping Jezebel!" said Leery. "He's a kid."

Dru sniffed. "He was nineteen."

"Yeah, that's what I said. A kid." Leery reached for the man's pockets, feeling for a wallet.

"Nice watch on his wrist," said Dru. "This wasn't a mugging."

"His zipper is down. Pants unbuttoned," said Leery. "At least he died happy." He glanced at Dru, who stared back without expression.

"It's not about sex for my mother's kind. That's only a lure to get what they need." She squinted at him. "Can we get by this?" she asked softly. "I can't change who I am any more than you can."

Leery shrugged his eyebrows. "Your mother's kind?"

She looked him dead in the eye. "That's right. The only way I could become your warder was to swear off sex." She tilted her head to the side. "What did you have to swear off to become a Claw?"

"Long pork," he muttered. "But I was trying to quit anyway—for religious reasons. Trust me when I say no kosher provider of human meat exists. Anywhere."

She cocked her head to the side and lifted one eyebrow. "I should hope not."

Leery shrugged and stooped to pull the man's wallet out of his stained back pocket. "Trusting soul," he murmured.

"ID?"

"Yeah." Leery straightened, wincing while he did so. "Nogan, meet Edward Thompson. Says here he's Irish." He glanced down at the man's fresh-faced good looks. "He came a long way to end up dead in Riverside Park."

"And that's weird by itself."

"Eh?"

"Most of my mother's subj—uh, *sisters*...operate closer to Times Square." She gave her little one-sided shrug without meeting his gaze. "Easier for them to fit in down there."

"You think they dragged this poor sap sixty blocks to dump him here? Why not use Central Park? It's closer and certainly bigger."

Nogan shrugged, this time using her left shoulder instead of her right. "Just telling you what I know to be true."

"You think this was something else? Maybe a spell to make it seem like the doings of a succubus?"

"Warder," she said. "Not a clairvoyant. Sorry."

"Right."

4

Butcher returned as Oriscoe and Nogan stepped back onto the tarmac path that twisted through the copse of trees inside the park. He lifted his chin at Oriscoe.

"Handle that for me, Butcher?" the detective asked.

"Sure thing," said Butcher. His gaze strayed to the stunning blonde Oriscoe had drawn as a partner. Some guys had all the luck, but Butcher wasn't one of those guys. His partner was a drunk who smelled like canned farts and alcoholism.

"Great!" said Oriscoe. "How about handling us a couple of coffees? I take mine regular. That means 'black' for the unlearned among us." He turned to his partner. "Nogan? How do you take your coffee?"

"Butcher has better things to do—"

"It's okay," said Butcher. "I'd rather walk than stand."

With her one-sided shrug, Dru said, "Black, seven sugars."

"*Seven?*" asked Oriscoe.

"A girl's gotta have *some* vices, Oriscoe." She turned and flashed a smile at Butcher hot enough to set his hair on fire.

"Cuh-cuh-coming right up." Butcher spun on his heel and started back up the path toward Riverside Drive.

"Oh, I think he likes you, Nogan."

"What's not to like?" She chuckled deep in her throat. "Let's see what the wits have to say."

"At least *they* won't be drooling all over themselves," muttered Leery as he strolled over to the women in running suits. "Ladies, I'm Leery Oriscoe, and this is my partner, Dru Nogan," he said in a louder voice. "Mind if we ask you a few questions?"

"We've already told the other cops everything we know," said the shorter of the two.

"Yeah, but we can't read their handwriting. Sorry, but you'll have to go through it again."

"No problem. I'm Kylelynn Fubelli, and this is Amie Brewer," said the taller of the pair.

"Out for a run?" asked Leery.

Brewer nodded, but Fubelli blushed to the roots of her hair and twirled her wedding band around her finger.

"Looking is okay. It's the touching that makes spouses antsy. Just ask my second wife."

Amie coughed to hide a chuckle. "Anyway, we'd only been here a few minutes before Ky saw the body."

"Right. And did you see anyone else? Anyone who looked out of place?"

The two women exchanged a glance and shook their heads.

"Are you sure? Someone hanging around acting in a suspicious way?"

"A woman, maybe?" asked Dru.

Again, the two women shared a glance and shook their heads.

"Great. One of these fine gentlemen in blue will get your contact information in case we need to speak to you again," said Leery, already turning away. "Where's Butcher with my coffee?"

"You'll have to excuse him. He's been a cop too long," said Nogan.

5

Fifty-five minutes later, Oriscoe and Nogan stepped out of Riverside Park across from 106th Street. Leery waved his hand toward 107th Street. "I've got the car up the block."

"I brought my own," said Dru. "I've got all my junk in it."

"You're not one of those cops who *decorates* their desk, are you?"

Dru laughed. "Not at all."

Leery looked at her askance. "No tchotchkes? No plants?" He drew a deep breath. "No *potpourri*?"

"Honest," said Nogan, raising her right hand.

Leery's gaze darted over her shoulder, and she turned to follow his glance. A garishly painted RV had pulled over to the curb a block away. The words "Mitzvah Tank" were emblazoned on its side, right next to the large portrait of a rabbi that bore the label, "Rabbi Zebbie Salman." With a nonplused expression on her face, Nogan turned back to Leery.

He was gone—walking back into the park at a rapid pace.

"Leery?" she called.

He lifted one hand to wave in unconscious mimicry of Jim Butcher. "Dropped something. Meet you at the house."

"Uh...okay."

CHAPTER 2

THE INVESTIGATION

I

Dru Nogan turned her back to the door of 10 Police Plaza and pushed it open with her ass. She carried a water-stained, crumbling cardboard carton in her hands.

In the lobby, she spun on her heel and strode through the "perp benches" toward the door that led to the elevators. The desk sergeant glanced at her, then did a double take, devouring her with his eyes.

"Help you, miss?" he asked.

She spared him a glance and a half-smile. "Special Investigations."

He cocked his head to the side and started to frown. "You…" He shook his head. "They get younger every year," he muttered.

She heard the mutter, though he voiced it low enough no one should have heard it. She owed her effect on men and the curved black horns emerging from her forehead to her mother's side of the family. Her augmented senses and occasional thirst for hot blood came from her father.

She tossed a wink at the desk sergeant and stepped to the interior of the Twenty-seventh Precinct, heading for the bank of elevators set aside for officer-use only. Stretching her thumb, she pressed the down button and stood waiting for the old elevator car to arrive.

Oriscoe's behavior there at the end struck her as strange—furtive, even—but he seemed like a cop with his shit together. She could work with that. Anxiety tickled her belly, but the cause of it wasn't anything Leery Oriscoe had said or done. No, it was the upcoming meeting with the squad's lieutenant.

Lieutenant Epatha Van Helsing was, by all accounts, an excellent cop and an even better commander, but she was a *Van Helsing*. The Van Helsing clan and her father's people didn't get along. Never had, never would.

On top of that, Epatha Van Helsing was a ghost. So, in addition to the intractable Van Helsing attitude about vampire-kind, her new lieutenant would, no doubt, be mired in her stubborn attachment to the past—to the time of her mortal death.

The bell dinged, and the elevator doors cracked open. The car was small and dirty, with what looked like puke smeared around in the corner. It smelled like a sty, and Dru dreaded being closed inside it, so she stood there glaring at it.

"Go ahead, Detective," said an ethereal voice in her ear. "You're not scared of a little puke, are you?"

Dru jumped a little but was proud of the fact she didn't gasp or enact some other melodrama. "Lieutenant Van Helsing?"

"I'm not the only ghost in the building, Detective." Van Helsing materialized behind her and to the left. She stood half a head shorter than Dru, but judging by her stern gaze, she was not intimidated in the least.

"Dru Nogan." She shifted the box to under her arm and held out her hand.

Van Helsing glanced down at it but made no move to take it. "Not yet," said the lieutenant. "First, I have to know you're not going to be a problem for me or my squad."

"What? Of course not!"

"Mmm-hmm." Van Helsing looked her up and down. "Your demonic tricks don't work on me, Nogan. Nor any ghost. Neither does the charm you no doubt inherited from your daddy."

Dru tried to suppress the sigh, but this scene had played itself out again and again throughout her admittedly short career. "I've taken the oaths."

Lieutenant Van Helsing waved her hand in front of her face as if dealing with an inappropriate odor. "Oaths can be broken"—she snapped her translucent fingers—"as easy as that."

"My word is good enough for the Chief of Ds."

"Yeah, well… Harry has always been swayed by swaying skirts. No doubt you gave him an eye full."

"Look, Lieutenant. I can't help my origins any more than you can help yours. I—"

"The quality of *my* family's heritage is known, doxy. *Your* family is made up of succubi and vampires. Neither race gives much credence to your word."

Dru set her jaw and stared fixedly at the pukey corner. "I've been a cop for eight years."

Van Helsing took a soundless step closer and peered up into Nogan's face. "And *that's* part of the problem, strumpet. Do you want to guess at how long I served in uniform before I made detective?"

"Lieutenant, I really—"

"Fourteen years, Nogan. And to earn my shield, I had to go to Vice. You know how many sickos live in this city?"

Dru shook her head.

"Well, it's a lot, and though many of them are mundanes, a significant number of them are not."

Nogan set her face in stone and waited for the lecture to end. Yes, she was young, but she'd worked hard to overcome the prejudices inherent in the magical justice system.

"Twenty-three."

She glanced at Van Helsing. "Twenty-three what?"

"Years. I had twenty-three years in before I made lieutenant. You look like you have twenty-three *minutes* on the job, yet here you are."

"Lieutenant D'Onofrio—"

"I read his report on you. What's more, I read what *wasn't* in his report. As far as I'm concerned, you bawdy little tart, you are a *liability* to your partner and the entire squad. You've got no business being a detective, let alone being assigned to The Supernatural Inquisition Squad. You have no experience under your belt. You think we spend our valuable time dealing with mundane crimes? You think your time reading meters has prepared you for anything?"

"That's not fair. I worked a beat, same as you."

"Maybe so," said Van Helsing with a dip of her chin. "For about ten minutes."

Frustration came on in the form of a stabbing headache. "Look, I'm here, so other people must disagree with you. I won't transfer out. I've worked too hard to get here."

"Oh, no, hussy... I don't think you want to take that attitude with me."

Dru sucked in a breath and let it dribble out. "I'm sorry. This is very frustrating. I hear the same thing over and over and over. When will—" She closed her mouth and shook her head.

"I'm sorry you're feeling out of sorts, trollop." Van Helsing turned away and then whirled back to face her. "No, I'm not. I'm glad to see the real you. I'm glad I could penetrate the sweet little girl façade you seem to have deployed on your other COs—your *male* COs, anyway."

"Obviously, you have a problem with me, but—"

"A problem with you, little minx? What I have a problem with is your leap-frogging career. Not because you're a woman, not even because you are a blood-sucking sex machine." Van Helsing raised a hand to wave away the inevitable protests. "No, what I have a problem with is the fact that you *know nothing* about the job in which you find yourself. You have none of the requisite skills, none of the necessary experience. You are a danger to every person in the squad, but, as you said, the Chief of Ds wants you here, so here you will stay. But allow me to tell you how it's going to be. You will learn what you need to know here, inside this building. You will gain the experience you lack while working with Oriscoe, following his lead, doing as he instructs you. Just don't think I'll allow you to step one foot outside this building alone until all that is corrected."

"But—"

"No, your bawdiness. This chat is finished." Van Helsing disappeared without another word, leaving Dru to fume and gag on the scent of old vomit.

"Whatever you say, Lieutenant," muttered Dru.

2

Leery entered the squad room fifteen minutes after Dru finished unpacking her carton of "desk junk." As he came in, Lieutenant Van Helsing stuck her head out of her office and waved them both inside.

Dru quirked her eyebrow at Leery, but he only smiled and motioned for her to go first. He swept off his camel hair overcoat and hung it on the squad's coat rack. Underneath, he wore a plain black suit, a white shirt, and a bad tie.

"You two get in here!" shouted Van Helsing.

"Uh-oh," said Leery. "She's in a mood."

"I might have something to do with that."

"Nah. The lieu's been in a bad mood for a century or more." He flashed his patented soothing smile at her.

"Well, I ran into her downstairs. Or rather, she appeared as I was just about to get on the elevator."

"Yeah, that's a neat trick, but I can see how it could be disconcerting the first time. She likes to—"

"There's more to it, Leery. What the hell kind of name is Leery, anyway?"

"What? I should go by 'Jeff' or a bullshit name like that? Tell me the 'more to it' part."

"You know about my mother."

"Yeah. So does the lieu."

"Yeah." Dru pulled a face, but even with her face all scrunched up like a pouting teenager's, she was beautiful. "She also knows about my dad."

Leery hitched a step and put his hand on her arm. "Your dad?"

Dru's nose twitched. "He's a vampire."

Leery's eyebrows shot upward, and he pulled his head back before whistling softly. "Damn, Nogan. You won the lottery on parents, didn't you?"

Dru grimaced. "Yeah." She glanced at Leery's face. "I don't suppose your parents—"

"Mom's Catholic, Dad's Jewish. That's about as mixed as I get."

"But your abilities…"

"I came by those on my own." He glanced at her and nodded. "Shapeshifter, you know. Werewolf." He tapped his chest. "But don't worry. I'm housebroken."

Dru grinned. She couldn't help it. Leery had a rough-around-the-edges charm.

"If you two are done, I'm waiting!" Van Helsing shouted through her office door.

Leery winked and strode into the office. "Morning, Lieu," he said. "Sorry, I'm running a little late. Nogan and I met at the scene in Riverside Park, but we had separate cars. I got caught in traffic, or I would have been here sooner."

"Shut up and sit down, Oriscoe," said the lieu, but she tipped him a wink and flashed a half-grin his way. When she turned to Dru, her face had hardened into a close approximation of granite. "*You* can stand."

Dru crossed her arms in front of her perfect breasts and stared at her shoes. "Whatever you say, Lieu."

"That's Lieutenant Van Helsing to you."

"Right. I'll remember that."

"Lieu, no one can pick their—" said Leery, but he stopped talking when Van Helsing held up her hand.

"No, Leery. I'll do the talking for a minute."

Leery nodded and tried to flash a reassuring grin at Dru, but she was staring at the floor with an almost ferocious intensity.

"We're stuck with the little cocotte here—at least until she screws up so bad that I can send her back to uniform. But I can't put her on the street...not and live with myself." Van Helsing sighed and sank into her desk chair. "Leery, you've got more experience than any ten Claws, but she's the only Warder I can assign you at the moment. You'll need to babysit her. She knows less than nothing, but no doubt thinks she got this whole thing wired for sound and lights."

"I don't—"

"Quiet now, jezebel. The adults are talking."

Dru shook her head but kept her lips together.

"Good. You learn quickly. That's a plus, as long as you are around long enough to learn what you need to know."

"Lieu, Nogan's okay. She was a real pro at the crime scene." He turned to see how Nogan was taking it.

Van Helsing raised both hands to her shoulders, palms out as though she'd like to push them both out of her office and be done with them. "Be that as it may, Leery, I've seen her file, and you haven't. She's worse than a rookie. Her rapid rise—no doubt due to her particular heritage and skills—has her thinking she knows it all. She's going to be over-confident. Your job will be to keep her in check." Van Helsing turned and looked him in the eye. "Teach her, Leery. Get her as ready for the street as you can. Until she *is* ready, though, she's not to leave the house unless shadowing you."

Leery returned his attention to Van Helsing and nodded. "No sweat, Lieu."

"Good. Now, tell me about your body."

"Nineteen-year-old male," said Leery. "From Ireland. He's been dried to a husk."

Van Helsing turned a glare on Dru. "Dried-out, huh?"

"Yeah. Probably ran into a succubus in Times Square, and it went bad."

Van Helsing nodded. "Is that what you think, chippie?"

Without raising her head, Dru shook it. "No. His body was found near the 106th Street entrance to Riverside Park. If it was a succubus from Times Square, how'd he get all the way over to the park?"

"I can think of a dozen ways," said Van Helsing. "The most likely of which is that a pet of the succubus who drained the victim's essence moved the body to protect his mistress."

"Could be," said Dru.

"But you don't think so."

Dru shrugged, still not looking at anyone.

"Mmm-hmm," said the lieutenant. "I suppose your upbringing gives you a particular insight." She tilted her head and gazed at Nogan. "Still. Cross the i's and dot the t's."

"I think you mean—"

"I said what I meant!" snapped Van Helsing. She glanced at Leery. "You two still here? Get to work."

"Right, Lieu." Leery rose and motioned toward the door. "Come on, Dru. Let me show you where the bad coffee is made."

3

Leery added seven sugars to Dru's cup and poured them both a cup from the filthy coffee maker. He grimaced as he took a sip. "Just like Mom used to make."

Dru sipped hers and, despite the sugar, couldn't stop herself from wincing.

"Yeah, the coffee's horrible. But on the plus side, I can only be killed by silver and magic. This doesn't qualify."

"Are you sure?" asked Dru. "Tastes like something an alchemist might use to clean off oxidation."

"Or clean drains."

"Or that."

Leery took another sip and treated her to another grimace. "Listen, kid. Don't take the lieu's attitude to heart. You're young, you're beautiful, and she might be able to forgive you for those two, but you're also half-vampire and half-demon. The Van Helsing clan—"

"I'm well aware of what the Van Helsings think of my kind."

Leery shrugged. "And plus, you're alive, and the lieu hasn't been alive for a long time. She gets a little jealous sometimes."

Dru nodded and peered into the black swill in her cup, looking for something living in there.

"And she does have a point. You *are* very young to have a gold shield, let alone be assigned to SIS. You know that."

"Yes, I do, Leery, but I worked hard to get here. I busted my ass—long hours, hard cases, no sleep, no food, my oath, all of it."

"Sure, sure. Lieu will come around. Don't worry about it."

Dru waved it away, then glanced at his face and cocked her head to the side. "Tell me."

"Tell you? What do you want me to tell you?"

"Why Leery? Why not use your name instead of a weird nickname?"

"Ha," said Leery. "I'll tell you because you're my partner, but I better not hear the mundanes talking about it."

"Not from me."

"Right. Leery is my real name." He shrugged. "Mom wanted Leonard; Dad wanted Jerome. They compromised with Leerome, which I hate, so Leery."

"Oh. What's embarrassing about that?"

"Not a thing as long as no one hears about it."

Dru nodded and took another horrible sip of coffee. "What is this stuff? Boiled shoes?"

Leery glanced at the coffee maker. "Nah. They save the good blends like that for special occasions.

Dru laughed, and it was husky, low in her throat.

"So... Fair is fair. Why Dru?"

"Short for Drusilla. Mom's a stickler for traditional names."

"Ah. And your dad didn't mind?"

Dru flashed a quirky grin. "Mom's a succubus, and Dad's a vampire, Leery. Their relationship is..."

"Complicated."

"Yeah, to say the least."

"I get it. Dad was a Black Hat who found himself a shiksa."

"Dad was a what who found himself a what?"

"Dad was Hassidic, Mom was a devout Catholic."

"Wow. I think I'd rather grow up as I did."

Leery shrugged. "They got along like peas in a pod. Maybe because of their different beliefs, they learned to compromise early in their relationship. By the time I burst onto the scene, they'd settled into their roles."

Dru lifted her chin and let it drop. "Which are you?"

"Which what am I?"

"Catholic or Jewish?"

"Ah. That would be telling." He wagged his eyebrows at her. "Come on, kid, let's go to work."

"Keep calling me 'kid,' and I'll have to start calling you 'Old Spice.'"

"Got it. 'Nogan' it is."

4

Leery pulled the cruiser into a spot about six inches too short for the length of the car and let the vehicle idle forward until the push bars rested against the bumper of the car in front. He gave it gas, and the back tires squealed a bit before the car in front started to slide forward.

"Nice parking job," said Dru with a chuckle.

"Yeah, it's a gift. Besides, if we pass by every space where someone else parks wrong in New York City, we'll never get anything done." Without bothering to back off the car's bumper, he put the unmarked cruiser in park and popped open his door. "Come on. The Irish Consulate to the United Nations is on the seventeenth floor. They should have information as to why our friend is here. I hope."

With an amused shake of her head, Dru got out of the car and followed Leery toward the stairs leading to the building's entrance.

"When we get inside, let me do the talking," said Leery. "Okay?" He cast a glance over his shoulder.

"Yeah, sure. I'll just stand there and bat my eyelashes at all the men."

"Hey, if it works..."

Dru rolled her eyes but said nothing.

They checked in with building security and flashed their IDs three or four times before they made it to the lobby of the consulate. On the wall behind the receptionist's desk, "*An*

Roinn Gnóthaí Eachtracha agus Trádála" was emblazoned in green. Beneath it, in the same shade, read, "Department of Foreign Affairs and Trade."

"Can I help you?" asked the receptionist, betraying his Irish roots with a mild accent.

"I hope so," said Leery. "An Irish citizen—a nineteen-year-old named Eddie Thompson—was murdered last night in Riverside Park."

"Ah, shame, that." The man behind the desk dipped his gaze for a moment. "What is it that brings you here?"

"We were hoping someone here might be able to give us a little information about the victim."

The receptionist sniffed. "Seems unlikely any of us would know the man." He picked up a pen and began to fiddle with it.

"That's right," said Leery. "But they have these things, now. Computers, they're called. Maybe you could click away at one and find the man's records."

The receptionist scoffed. "You can read the wall behind me, can't you? I doubt very much that a nineteen-year-old is part of the Trade Mission."

"Sure, I get that, but they have this other thing called the Internet that connects computers in various places. An information superhighway, they say. Perhaps you could flag down a tiny bit of that information blipping by at the speed of light in another branch of your government."

The man leaned back in his chair and folded his arms over his chest. "There are proper channels for fecking information requests."

"Look, we can easily get a—"

Dru stepped past Leery and smiled at the receptionist. The man's mouth dropped open, and Leery closed his own, as it seemed clear the man no longer knew he was there. "Can't you help us, sir?" Dru's voice sent a ripple of electric sexual energy up and down Leery's spine. The receptionist seemed to melt into the chair, and his eyes almost glazed.

"Jeanie Mac," the receptionist murmured. "Aren't you just deadly pretty?"

"Thank you. Can you help me?" She took a subtle step in front of Leery, blocking the receptionist's view.

"I'd be as happy as Larry to help you, dearie. What was the lad's name again?"

"Eddie Thompson," said Dru. "Edward."

"Right. Let's just see what the story is." He bent forward over his computer keyboard and clacked away. After a few moments, he peeked at Dru. "Says here Mr. Thompson is from The Pale. Are you sure the name is right?"

"Yes," said Dru. "What's 'The Pale?'"

"Oh. The Pale is the region near Dublin. It says here the lad applied to come to New York to take in the sights. On holiday, then. Out to be a lad in a big city. Probably on the tear and ran afoul of someone. How'd he die?"

"We don't know for sure. There are tests to be run, and an autopsy in the works."

"Ah," said the receptionist. He clacked away for a moment or two, then leaned forward and peered at the screen. "This can't be bang on. The stupid thing must be banjaxed."

"What is it?" asked Dru.

"Stupid box says he's got a relative in the City."

"Okay. What's this relative's name?"

"Fiona Rae Gill." The receptionist shook his head and swatted the side of his computer. "Fecking thing's broken."

"Do you have an address for Ms. Gill?" asked Dru.

"Yes," said a woman's voice from behind them. "And you're standing in my lobby. I'm Fiona Rae Gill, Irish Ambassador to the United Nations."

"Oh, boy," muttered Leery, turning to gaze at the woman in a nice suit.

"Why are you looking for me? What's this all about?"

"Ambassador," said the receptionist. "There must be a mistake. The computer says..." He quit talking, staring at the ambassador with a confused expression on his face.

"Are you related to Edward Thompson?" asked Leery.

The ambassador's gaze bounced from the receptionist to Leery and finally settled on Dru. "And who is this fine thing?"

"NYPD, ma'am. I'm Detective Oriscoe. This is my partner, Detective Nogan."

Rae Gill's gaze remained fixed on Dru. "And what's wee Eddie gotten himself into now?"

"Maybe you should sit down," said Leery.

The ambassador turned a blank gaze his way and shook her head. "Tell it to me straight."

"We found Mr. Thompson this morning in Riverside Park."

"Bah! What's the thick lad gotten into now?"

"You knew he was in the City?" asked Nogan.

"Yes. He came to have one last gas and to go on the lash a bit."

"Um…"

"He came to have a bit of fun and go drinking. He's to be married next month. So, what's the charge?"

"The charge, ma'am?"

"You said you had my nephew, Eddie. Picked him up in a park, you said."

Leery treated her to a half-shake of his head. "We said we *found* him in Riverside Park. I'm afraid someone murdered your nephew last night."

Ambassador Gill shifted her gaze back and forth between Leery and Dru, her face flat and expressionless. "Tell me you're taking the piss," she said after a few moments of silence.

"No, Ambassador," said Leery in a quiet, respectful voice. "I'm afraid not."

"That little eejit!" she hissed and closed her eyes. "His mother will never speak to me again." She opened her eyes after two breaths, and when she did, she was all business. "He always was a chancer. Had the luck of the devil, that one did." She turned to Leery and stepped closer. "Tell me what you haven't said yet."

Leery glanced at Dru, then took a breath. "It seems he ran into trouble with a..."

"With a what, Detective?"

"We don't know anything for sure, but we have evidence he was with a sex worker."

"A floozie? Yes, that sounds like something that fecking eejit would do. Come to New York to dip his wick one last time before taking his vows and settling down to married life." She squinted at Leery. "Perhaps we can keep that part quiet? This holy show will break his mot's heart."

"I can't promise it won't get out, but it won't come from us."

Ambassador Gill nodded once and turned her attention to the receptionist. "Danny?"

"Of course, Madam Ambassador. My lips are sealed."

"Did Eddie have friends in the City?"

Fiona frowned and shook her head. "Not from back home. Maybe from his ten minutes at Uni."

"He quit school?"

"Said it wasn't for him, but we know he spent most of his time bunking off or ossified or both." She hitched a sigh. "Do you think this floozie he was with killed him?"

"It looks like that," said Leery. "It's all subject to what the ME finds."

"Must I identify his body?" Fiona asked in a small voice.

"Eventually," said Dru. "But it's probably a technicality. We found his ID on him, and he matches the picture."

Gill closed her eyes and sighed. "Aye."

"We'll need to retrace his movements. Track down how he spent his time and with whom."

"But I don't know the answer to those questions."

"How about where he went? Is there a bar close to your residence that he liked?"

The ambassador turned to the receptionist. "Danny? I know he asked you for recommendations."

Danny gazed up at her with almost glazed eyes. His lips twitched several times before he spoke. "Yeees."

Dru narrowed his eyes at the man, who squirmed under her scrutiny. "You acted as if you didn't know him."

"I…" He shook his head, looking genuinely confused. "I mistook him for another Eddie Thompson, I guess. It didn't dawn on me that—"

"It's a common enough name," said the ambassador.

"And?" asked Leery. "Which clubs did you point out to him?"

An expression of sick horror passed across the man's face. "I did more than recommend. I also took him out a few times. Introduced him to a few ladies…" He stole a glance at Fiona's face. "And a couple of good bars."

"The type of bar where the waitresses dance on a small stage next to a chrome pole? A place where maybe the women forget to get dressed?"

Danny ducked his head. "Yeah."

"Near Times Square?"

"Yeah."

"And last night?" asked Leery. "Did you take him out?"

"No, not last night."

"Why didn't you tell us this right away?" asked Dru.

Danny's face turned crimson, and he dropped his gaze to his lap. "I…" He took a deep breath. "I thought it had to be a mistake, maybe another Eddie Thompson, like I said."

Dru flipped open her leather-bound pad and slapped it on the desk in front of the blushing man. She lay her gold Cross pen diagonally across the paper. "Names and addresses of these strip joints you and Eddie visited."

"And anywhere else you might have taken him. Somewhere that's maybe a bit more extreme than a nudie-bar."

Danny swallowed hard as he picked up Dru's pen and began to write. "I didn't think anything would happen. He just wanted to have one last hurrah—a place to get fluthered while taking a gander at beautiful women. I didn't know this would happen."

"Write," said Dru in an arctic voice.

When Danny finished, he passed the pad back to Dru without meeting her gaze. "Ambassador Gill, I'm so sorry. I never—"

"No, of course not," said Fiona. "How could you know something like this would happen?"

Leery stepped closer to the desk and peered down at the list as Danny added the names of strip clubs to it. "Huh. You took him to all these places? Some of them are bad news, and you should have known something *could* happen. Anyone who's visited them knows it."

Danny hung his head. "Yeah, but Eddie…" He stole a shame-faced glance at the ambassador. "Eddie wanted a little raunch."

"It's okay, Danny," said the ambassador. "You didn't mean any harm."

Leery arched an eyebrow at Dru but said nothing.

"That's the whole list? You haven't held anything back to spare the ambassador's feelings?"

Danny shook his head. "That's all of them. I only went out with him a few times. I don't know what else he might have found on his own."

"Fine. Add your contact information to the bottom there."

Danny wrote on the pad before passing the pen back to Dru. She picked up her pad and tucked it away. She gazed at Leery for a moment, and he treated her to a small shake of his head. She frowned before turning to the ambassador. "Ambassador, you seem very understanding of Danny's role in your nephew's demise. One might imagine you aren't surprised to hear any of this."

Fiona Rae Gill narrowed her eyes and glared at Dru coldly. "If there's one thing my years of public service have taught me, Detective, it's that everyone reacts differently. I've been trained to keep a cool head—I couldn't be much use as an ambassador if I were ruled by my emotions."

Dru lifted her chin, gazing back with open suspicion.

"Thanks for your help, Ambassador," said Leery. "We've got everything we need for now. We'll reach out when we get a better picture of what happened."

"Fine." Gill brushed past them and stepped into the inner offices of the ministry.

"Come on, *partner*," said Leery. "Let's see if we can verify Danny's story." He turned and exited the lobby, holding the door for Dru and taking one last look at Danny, who sat with his head in his hands.

"What?" asked Dru.

"Do you drive everywhere with your siren blaring and your lights spinning?" he asked quietly.

"My siren…"

"Yeah. Do you always let everyone know what you think, what you intend to do?"

"I... Something's not right in there." She hooked her thumb at the Trade Ministry. "Trained or not, that's one cold fish."

Leery raised his eyebrows but nodded. "Yeah, it was strange, but now she *knows* you thought it was strange. She knows she needs to do a better acting job next time. She'll be on guard."

"Oh," said Dru in a small voice. "I—"

"You did good with Danny. Your instinct was dead on there."

"Thanks. I should have stopped when I was ahead."

"Sometimes, it's better to leave things unsaid, unnoticed. There's a time for frank confrontation, and there's a time for subtlety."

"Right." Dru stood looking down at her expensive shoes. "Are you going to tell the lieutenant?"

"Have to, Nogan. She'll hear about it, anyway. I swear the woman has a spy ring to rival the CIA. Anyway, it'll help."

"How? How can that help?"

"I bet you'll be more circumspect next time, right?" Leery gazed at her until she nodded. "Van Helsing will see the progress. She'll see you learning and relax a little." He cracked a smile. "To be honest, I was planning on telling her a lie if you made it through without a mistake."

"You were going to lie and say I screwed up, even if I didn't?"

Leery laughed at her expression. "Trust me, Dru, I once played a doctor in a school play."

5

Thirty minutes later and twenty blocks away, Leery repeated his parking method, this time pushing a white delivery van forward.

"Doesn't anyone ever complain?" asked Dru.

"Nah. I put a card on the window. Nothing like getting a homicide detective's card stuck to your window to drive away thoughts of complaining. Most people take the card and quietly disappear into the shadows."

Nogan's gaze traveled to the blinking red neon sign that read "NUDE-NUDE-NUDE" and curled her lip in a sneer. Her eyes bounced to the next club, one that advertised "A

GIRLFRIEND EXPERIENCE FOR THE DISCERNING GENTLEMAN" in big purple neon letters. The last door on the block was painted fire engine red, but there was no sign. "What's that one?"

Leery glanced at the red door. "That is a club named by the most creative sleazeball in New York. It's called 'The Red Door.'"

"Doesn't need to advertise?"

Leery shook his head. "No, I don't guess they do. It caters to a certain crowd—even supernaturals frequent the place." A slow grin spread across his face. "Let's start there." He straightened his bad tie and drew his overcoat tight around his torso.

"Um, okay."

Leery pushed the door open hard, letting it bang against the inside wall. He strode in, bold as brass, a wide grin plastered on his face. "Freeze! This is a raid!"

The bartender glanced over and rolled his eyes. "Raid, my ass, Leery."

"Yeah, but I've always wanted to say that." Leery glanced at Nogan and pointed at the back with his head. "I'm going over there to talk to Mr. Creative. Why don't you head back to the dressing room and ask if anyone remembers him?"

"Why? Because I'm a woman?"

"No, because you're half-succubus and half-vampire. Mr. Creative over there will pop a gasket, and even if he doesn't, we won't be able to understand him for all the drool and blubbering."

Dru scowled and nodded. "Yeah, okay."

Leery watched her picking her way to the darkened recesses of the seedy little bar, shaking his head a little as every male head in the place turned to mark her progress. She seemed oblivious to the scrutiny, but Leery had the idea she'd had people staring and drooling at her all her life.

"What the hell is this, Oriscoe?" demanded the bartender.

"Don't get your knickers in a wad, MacPherson. I'm coming." Leery glanced at the dancers and smiled as he walked. None of them were supernaturals. "Listen here, MacPherson. You get a kid—"

"No kids. It's not that type of place."

"Relax, MacPherson. Relax. I said 'kid,' I meant 'young man.' Fresh-faced, Irish accent, nineteen years old. He came in earlier in the week with another young man, also Irish, but probably came back alone last night." Leery leaned across the bar. "Came back looking to *play*."

"The Red Door is a—"

Leery growled deep in his chest. "I know what The Red Door is, MacPherson. Right now, I'm pretending I don't, but if you want to play hardball..."

MacPherson held up his hands in surrender. "No, no. Let's go into my office." He snapped his fingers at a bombshell blonde working the other end of the bar, then turned and led Leery into a small hallway near the bar. He stopped at the first door and fished his keys out of his pocket, then stepped into the dark room.

He left the lights out—probably an attempt to keep him off balance—but Mr. Creative didn't know about Leery's darker half. He could see just fine in the light from the bar.

The bare-walled and spartan office smelled of body odor and worse. MacPherson's desk was a cheap metal-job—probably government surplus—and none of the other furniture had been new for at least twenty years.

Without being asked, Leery slipped into one of the visitor's chairs and swung a foot up on the desk, all without making a sound. "Now, you were going to tell me about the kid."

MacPherson's office chair creaked as he sank into it, and he grinned an evil little grin as he reached for a small electrical switch box on his desk. He flipped a switch, and hot, white light washed the room. His gaze was centered on the wall over Leery's shoulder—at the place where he expected Oriscoe to be standing.

Leery chuckled as the man's gaze tracked to him, and MacPherson's face fell a little. "If we're done with the games, we can get down to it, MacPherson."

The man scowled and tossed the remote light switch box back onto his desk. "Get your feet off," he muttered.

Leery didn't move a muscle, just went on staring at the other man's face as if it were a feature on a particularly ugly bug. "The kid?"

"Yeah, yeah, yeah." MacPherson leaned back, his chair squealing and creaking. "I saw him. He came in a few days back with a semi-regular. A man."

"Right. Danny."

MacPherson hit him with a quick nod. "Sure, Danny. Came in about ten, watched a few shows, drank a bit, then left sometime after midnight."

"And last night?" Leery kept his voice friendly, but his nostrils flared at the scent of the other man's fear.

"No. Neither of them came in last night."

"You mean Danny didn't come in, but the kid, Eddie Thompson, he came in by himself."

"No, I told you—"

Leery's chest rumbled with what was unmistakably the feral growl of a wolf. He swung his foot to the floor, moving it slowly and with an economy of movement that would make a dancer envious. "Should I get up, MacPherson?" he asked in a voice as soft as silk.

"Listen, Oriscoe, I don't know what your game is, but—"

With a snarl, Leery leaned forward, slapping his hands on the desk. His lips rippled back to reveal his sharp-looking canine teeth. "My game, you fat asshole? Do I look like I'm playing with you?"

MacPherson swallowed hard, his gaze crawling from Oriscoe's mouth to his eyes and back again. "Listen, I don't want any trouble with one of your kind."

"A homicide detective, you mean?" asked Leery, relaxing back into the chair and letting his voice turn friendly once more. "Yeah, we can be a pain in the ass."

MacPherson swallowed again and nodded. "Yeah." He dropped his gaze to the desk's scarred and time-worn top, then cleared his throat. "And as for the other thing, the thing I know nothing about, I say, 'live and let live.'"

Leery tipped him a wink. "A wise policy, but can we get back to the kid? He came in last night, didn't he? And he left with someone...*special*. Someone you apply your live-and-let-live policy to."

MacPherson kept his eyes downcast. He cleared his throat and drew a deep breath. "In my profession, sometimes you come across information that is... I mean, you meet certain people who..." He grimaced.

"Yeah. Being a purveyor of adult entertainment—and sometimes a little more—you ran across a group of...*women*, let's say...who have a unique ability to part men from their money." Leery hooked his thumb toward the hallway. "And not the regular ability to part suckers from dollar bills. These women make the others look like girls on the playground. Am I right?"

"Yeah."

"And you being an entrepreneur, you naturally wanted to use their skillset to your advantage, so you proposed a deal?"

MacPherson nodded after a quick peek at Leery's expression. "Sure. Why not?"

"Why not, indeed?" Leery smiled and held his hands out to his sides. "And remember, I'm with homicide. I don't give a rat's ass about the scams those Vice cops want to run on you. I don't care if you take a cut from the, uh, extracurricular activities of your girls. All I care about is murder."

MacPherson sighed with relief. "Yeah. Okay."

Leery lifted both palms upward. "Then we've got that out of the way. Now, you can feel comfortable telling me anything."

"Unless I murdered the little prick," muttered MacPherson.

Leery chuckled. "Trust me, MacPherson. You've got the wrong set of parts for what killed poor Eddie. It was a real live-and-let-live evening, I'm sure."

The fat club-owner blushed and scratched his chest. "You want to talk to Deli."

"'Deli?' Should I order a pastrami sandwich?"

"Delilah Lara is her name." MacPherson lifted his fat shoulders and let them fall. "Goes by 'Deli' on stage. You know, the place you want to eat."

"Yeah, I got that." Leery stood. "And Deli's here today?"

MacPherson hooked his thumb over his shoulder. "Dressing room, probably. She's supposed to dance in thirty."

"I've always wondered why it's called a *dressing room* in nudie bars," Leery said with a grin. "Seems like an oxymoron." MacPherson didn't look up, didn't respond, so Leery turned to leave.

"Oriscoe, I got nothing to worry about from you, right?"

Leery turned back and let a little of his dark half show in his face. His lips stretched and peeled back, revealing all of his teeth. "Why would I want to...*bother* such a forward thinker as you?" He slid his long tongue out between his teeth and ran it across his lips.

"You know, a guy with a live-and-let-live outlook and all."

MacPherson gulped and seemed ready to shrink under his desk.

"You might want to reconsider your hiring practices, though. Deli's burned the golden goose." He turned and walked into the hall before he allowed himself to chuckle.

6

Dru picked her way through the public area of the strip club and found the door to the dancers' dressing room. She slipped through the door, feeling the stare of every single man in the club.

"Oh, honey, you could *clean up* here," said a mezzo-soprano voice that reminded Dru of Ella Fitzgerald's. "But those clothes would have to go." The voice came from a beautiful dark-skinned woman wearing a sequined dress and impossibly high-heeled shoes.

"I'm not here to dance."

The woman laughed. "Oh, honey, we're *all* here to dance, only some of us recognize that, and some don't." She shrugged her shoulders and laughed again.

Dru found herself warming to the woman's friendly manner and warm laughter, even if there was something a little off about the woman. She grinned. "In this case, I'm really not *here* to dance. I'm Detective Dru Nogan from the Two Seven."

The woman flashed a bemused smile and turned her head a little, lifting an eyebrow. "I've never seen a cop who looked like you, honey. Are you sure you don't want to try a dance?"

"I'm sure."

The woman sighed and shrugged. "Our loss, then. What can I do for you, Detective?"

Dru fished the picture of Eddie Thompson out of her pocket and held it out toward the woman. "Did you run into a young Irish man here last night?"

The woman continued to stare into Dru's eyes, a small smile on her lips. "I don't look much at the men who come in here. They bore me."

"This is important."

"Just what sort of cop are you?"

"Homicide," said Oriscoe, pushing his way through the door. "Are you Deli?"

The woman glanced at Leery and looked him up and down.

"I thought you didn't look at men," he said with a smile.

"Men, no. Wolves? Oh-my-yes." Her eyes twinkled, and she fluttered a hand in front of her chest.

"Alas, I'm here to work," said Leery.

Dru watched their banter, paying particular attention to the woman. "Are you Deli?" she asked.

"No, honey," said the woman, turning her gaze on Dru. "Deli called in sick. You can call me 'Ella.' Everyone does."

"What, because of your voice?" asked Oriscoe.

"No, because that's my name. Oh, not the name my mama blessed me with, but I've always hated that one."

"Oh? And what name did your mother give you?"

"Eugenia."

"Ah," said Leery. "Ella it is."

Ella laughed and laid her delicate hand on Leery's arm. "Aren't you just the dickens. Growl for me, sexy."

"Maybe later," said Leery.

"Who's your mother, Eugenia?" asked Dru, her voice hard.

Ella turned to her and smiled. "Took you long enough," she murmured. "You wouldn't know her, honey. She's from South Africa."

"Wait, what?" asked Leery.

"And why are you here?" demanded Dru. "Here, I mean. Dancing in this club."

Ella smiled and batted her eyelashes. "We don't all have the connections to get straight jobs."

Dru's face wrinkled. "It doesn't take connections, Eugenia. It takes desire and commitment."

"Oh, I've got desires, honey," said Ella, stepping close to, but not touching Dru. "A beautiful thing like you brings 'em right up to the top."

"Oh, I get it," said Leery. "She's a succubus, right?"

"Glad you could catch up," said Dru. "Yeah, she's one of my mother's people."

"A girl needs to make a living, sweetie Nothing wrong with what I do here. Flesh is flesh, and we all have an unending supply of it."

"Except the undead," said Leery.

"And the men you deal with?" demanded Dru. "I suppose you never turn up the heat to get more money stuffed in your G-string? Never smile in that special way?"

"A woman's got to use what the good Lord gave her."

"Thought so."

"Hey, hey. Let's all be friends here," said Leery. "We're not here to cause problems for you, Ella. We just need to know where we can find the one they call Deli."

"Aw, I was looking forward to you causing me problems, wolfman."

"Cut it out!" snapped Dru. "Turn it off before I slap cuffs on you."

Ella chuckled and held out her wrists. "Cuffs? Oh-my-yes. Whatever straightens your kinks, I always say."

Dru scoffed and rolled her eyes. "Come on, Oriscoe. She's not going to help us."

"Oh, honey, don't give up so easily! Can't a girl play hard to get?"

"Sure she can," said Leery. "Up to a point."

"Ah ha. And we've reached that point, wolfie?"

Leery tilted his head to the left. "I'm not much on nicknames, Ella, and, yes, we have reached that point. Deli's address?"

"Well, then." Ella beamed at Leery for a heartbeat, then turned her gaze on Dru. "Who's got a pad and paper?"

7

With Deli's home address in hand, Dru and Leery let The Red Door swing shut behind them and went out on the sidewalk. "Say... You don't think..."

"She's a succubus, Leery."

"Well, yeah, I know. But don't you date?"

Dru smirked. "Me or Ella?"

"Any of you."

"Of course, we date. But only people who can handle it. You know, vampires, incubi, the immune."

"Wait, people are immune to your, uh, charms?"

"Sure. They're rare, but the immune do exist."

"Interesting." His eyes darted back to the door of the club.

Dru scoffed and gave him a single shake of her head. "She's not interested, Leery. She's *hungry.* She was hitting on *me* before you came in, and she'd already sussed out my nature."

"She could, uh, feed on you?"

Dru shrugged as if the prospect didn't matter to her at all. "Sure, she just can't charm me."

Leery turned back to her, a strange expression on his face. "Then, you'd have to let her."

"Correct. That's why she was hitting on me. She was...how do you men say it? She was putting up her flag."

"Ah." Oriscoe turned back to the club. "Maybe I should get her number..."

"She'd eat you for lunch, Oriscoe. Literally."

Leery chuckled. "All the smooth chocolate skin. It might be worth it."

"Do you want to end up like Eddie Thompson? A dried-out husk? Because that's what my Magic 8-Ball says is in your future if you go back in there." Dru sighed and glanced at the car. "Plus, she's a thousand years old or so. If you like older women, I can grab a cab back to the station. You can come get me when you are...done."

Leery threw one last glance at The Red Door, then put his back to it. "Nah. A guy can dream, though, right?"

"Well..."

"Yeah, I know. I didn't mean the sleeping kind." He hitched a sigh and pointed at the next club down the line. "Feel like a 'girlfriend experience?'"

Dru tapped the pocket of her coat, where she kept her pad. "We've already got Deli's information."

"Sure we do, but she might not be the succubus we want. Danny said he took Eddie to all these clubs, right?"

"Right."

"Then we dot our t's and cross our eyes." He crossed his eyes, and Dru grunted. "Come on, Druscilla. We've got work to do."

"Don't call me that!" she snapped. "Or I have to call you 'Leerome.'"

"Like I said, we've got work to do, Dru."

"That's what I thought." She glanced at the flashing neon signs. "Christ, I hope we don't find anything."

"Squeamish, Nogan?" asked Leery. "Stick with me, kid. We'll make this as painless as pulling off a band aid."

"That always hurts way more than you think it will."

8

Leery swung the unmarked car into another spot that was too small for the car, pushing a Honda forward until its tires hopped up on the curb, then backing up a foot. "There," he said with satisfaction. "Perfect fit."

"You're a nutjob, Leery," murmured Dru.

"Sure, but I'm just a conflicted New York Jew who got hit by the Hassidic bus—only the bus was driven by a werewolf. There's bound to be a little crazy under my hat."

"Maybe, but you're a lot crazy."

Leery shrugged and smiled. "Would you want a Claw that wasn't?"

"You've got a point." She glanced up at the Upper West Side brownstone Delilah Lara called home. "How do you want to handle this?"

"With my usual charm and good looks."

"Right. I'll do the talking then?"

"You might just make it in this racket, Dru." Leery opened his door without checking for traffic and climbed out. "Come on, Nogan. Let's go talk to her."

Dru got out on the sidewalk and glanced at Leery across the roof of the car. "Maybe I should go in alone."

"Not a chance, slick." Leery slammed his door and came around the front of the car.

"Just remember she can make you think she's anyone with her charm. She can convince you that lying down so she can suck the life out of you is *exactly* why you came."

"I *have* done this before, Dru." He flashed a smile at her. "Just don't let me make a fool of myself."

"That's going to be difficult."

Leery threw back his head and laughed.

They mounted the stoop, and Leery knocked on the door. "Pretty fancy for a stripper."

Dru cocked her head. "Maybe she's as old as Ella."

"Old money, huh? Then why strip?"

"A girl's gotta eat." Dru flipped her hair out of her face. "This wind sucks."

"Speaking of eating... You hungry? Want to grab a bite after this?"

"Half-succubus, half-vampire." She looked him in the eye. "Those fleabag dumps we spent all morning in gave me more than enough."

"Oh, right." He knocked again, harder this time. "Too bad everything after The Red Door was a waste of time. I told you they would be."

Dru stared at him for a moment, then chuckled. "Do you make a joke of everything, Oriscoe?"

"I try. Look, half-Catholic, half-Jew, and that's before we even mention the werewolf part. It's not like I can take the world seriously."

"Touché."

"Maybe she's not home." Leery tried to peer through the cut glass window in the door, but all he could see were vague shapes and white upon white. A few splotches of bright pastel colors littered the fuzzy landscape. "Looks like a polar bear in a blizzard in there. How the hell would you keep all that white clean?"

"I've got a funny feeling, Leery," muttered Dru. "Like we're being watched. Or..." She put her hand to her forehead and rubbed between her brows.

"Funny feeling like something's about to happen? Yeah, I've got that, too." He unbuttoned his camelhair coat, slipped out of it, and held it out to Dru. "Hold this for a second? Just in case."

She raised her eyebrows and looked at him.

"What, I should ruin my good coat for this shiksa?"

Dru rolled her eyes but took the coat with her free hand as Leery banged on the door.

"Hear that, Dru?"

"Hear what?"

"Do you hear that woman screaming?"

"I don't hear anyone screaming."

"*Listen* again. I'm sure you'll hear her."

"Look, Oriscoe, I know what you're trying to do, but I'm already in trouble with Van

Helsing, and it's my first day for crying out loud."

Leery wagged his head to the side. "Okay, okay. Then we wait."

"For what? She's either not home or not coming to the door."

"Right. We wait for her to come out or come home." He turned, snatched his coat out of her hands, and glanced up and down the street. "We're going to need coffee."

9

Leery dozed in the passenger seat of the car, a bit of drool making his lips glisten in the afternoon sun. Dru eyed the five empty coffee cups on the dash in front of him—the five *ultra grande* cups. "Don't know how you can sleep after all that caffeine, Oriscoe," she murmured.

"Don't know how I can sleep with you yapping, either."

"You're drooling on your lapels."

"Occupational hazard," he said without opening his eyes. "Need more coffee?"

"More? I haven't had any at all."

"Right. Need more coffee." Leery opened his eyes and ran his hand over his lips, then his lapels. "Anything?"

"The mailman came at three, kids from the school up the street walked by, the UPS man. That's it."

Leery glanced at his watch and grimaced. "I always catch cases like this when I have tickets to the Jets."

"It's not football season."

"Yeah, I know. Just saying if I ever get Jets tickets, expect a long day." He rubbed his eyes, then stretched them open wide. He squinted at Deli's brownstone. "Should we go knock again?"

"If you think it will help."

"It won't, but it's something to do." Leery grinned at her, putting his hand on the door handle.

"So is sitting here," Dru said with a one shouldered shrug.

"Right." Leery reached for his latest coffee cup and shook it. "Perfect." He threw the coffee cup back onto the dash, then settled back to wait, watching the sky color and darken as dusk fell.

Dru rocked forward, squinting her eyes to see through the gloom and staring through the windshield. "Look at that."

"What? Deli?" He followed her gaze.

A woman came up from the basement apartment of Deli's building. She was swathed in black from head to toe and had a backpack thrown over one shoulder. After glancing up and down the street, she dropped her head and started walking away from the car.

"Let's go," said Leery. He got out and walked toward the black-clad woman at a rapid pace. "Excuse me!" he called. "Ms. Lara? I have some important papers for your review."

The woman in black stopped and turned to face them slowly. She lifted a hand as if to wave and then sprinted up the alley by her side.

"Great, a foot chase," said Leery. "I just *love* to run."

"Then you shouldn't have called out to her."

"There's always a critic around at times like this." Leery stopped walking, then turned back and popped open the trunk. He stripped off his camel hair coat and threw it in the trunk. He reached inside and grabbed a wide-brimmed black hat made from heavy wool. "Hold this," he said as he tossed his hat to Dru. "Just in case."

Dru looked at the black woolen hat in her hand and shook her head. "Is this like a mortal woman handing her purse to her husband?"

"That's what my first wife used to do. All the time." He unbuttoned his shirt, already starting to change.

"What am I supposed to do with this?" she asked, looking down at the hat. When she raised her eyes, Leery's face had distended, and thick, coarse hair had sprung up all over his body. He dropped his shirt into the trunk and reached for the clasp of his belt. "Oh, right," she said.

"If I have to run, I might as well be fast," Leery grated. "Watch my back. Oh, and put this junk in the car." He stepped out of his trousers.

Dru nodded, scooped up his pants and shoes, then turned to throw them in the trunk.

"Not the hat!" Leery came toward her, holding out his hand—a hand tipped with savage claws and wrapped in brownish-gray fur the same color as his human hair.

As Dru watched, the hair atop his head wove itself into a yarmulke, and he settled his hat over it. A set of magnificent, glossy *payot* hung from the sides of his head.

His change complete, Leery stood a foot taller than his human half. The skin on his long snout wrinkled, and his lips curled, showing his long, sharp fangs. A growl erupted deep in his chest, and he took a half-step toward her.

"Whoa, big fella. The *other* succubus fled down that alley. I'm your partner!"

If anything, his snarl turned even more vicious as his hackles rose all down his back. His ears lay back against his lupine skull, and he glared at her through narrowed eyelids.

"Go on!" she snapped. "Go after the *criminal* succubus!"

He snarled at her a final time, then turned and loped toward the alley. Every few steps, he lifted his nose to catch Deli's scent on the wind.

Dru stood next to the car for a heartbeat, watching his massive muscles bunching under his furred skin and shivered at the idea of those muscles driving his savage claws into her skin. She shook herself and tossed the rest of Leery's clothes into the car. The werewolf rounded the corner into the alley without slowing, running on the wall for a few steps before dropping back to the bricks. She sprinted to get to the corner, trying to keep him in sight.

With her right hand, she sketched a rune in the air, which glowed neon red. She slid around the corner and drew more runes in a circle around the first. She muttered the word of power that would give the ward its life, then cast it at Leery's retreating back.

At the other end of the alley, Leery howled and snarled.

10

Leery stretched out his stride, luxuriating in the feeling of freedom that came with his change. His hat kept trying to fly off his head. He growled at the black wool as he pushed it farther down over his lupine skull. The hat creaked as it stretched to fit. He went through four or five hats a month because he kept ripping them open, trying to wedge them further on his skull. A ward settled around his shoulders with a tingle and pop, and the Black Hat wolf in him howled and snarled.

Settle down! She's doing her job, bozo. That's a protective ward from our new partner. I didn't even have to ask for it.

Delilah's scent trail filled his nostrils like blinking over-amped neon signs, and he couldn't help but notice the musk of sex permeating it all. He sprinted across the next street over and into the darkened alley beyond, leaving Dru to follow as best she could.

As he bolted down the garbage-strewn alley in total silence, his gaze jumped from shadow to shadow, from hiding place to hiding place. *She must know we're SIS*, he thought. *Or at least assume that. I would, in her place. Gotta be ready for anything.*

He leaped over a black jacket, and a few steps later, a black knit winter hat. The stuff reeked with Deli's sweat and fear. Leery left them where they lay, leaving them for Dru to collect and bag into evidence.

Must be getting close to her. There's no way a succubus can outrun me—she has to know that. Leery breezed across another sidewalk and another empty street, not needing to look around to know which way the woman ran, nor to know that no cars would smash into him as he crossed the road. Sometimes he envied his human senses. At least he didn't have to smell the constant stink of exhaust, body odor, shit, and plastic.

Deli had tried to get cute at the entrance to the next alley. Her scent trail dipped into the shadow-cloaked alley, but after running five steps or so, she'd turned back and raced around the corner and down the sidewalk. If werewolves could smirk, Leery would have as he skipped the attempted misdirection and jumped straight to the new path across the concrete.

It was a risk, to go running down a twilit street populated by mundanes just as bold as brass, but Leery didn't hesitate. There was always something in the tabloids for a day or so, and then it was replaced by the next mutant baby or celebrity break-up. Of course, the traditional press didn't cover any werewolf sightings in Upper West Side.

Lara's scent trail raced up the stoop of another anonymous brownstone and disappeared inside. Leery glanced over his shoulder, hoping to see Dru coming out of the alley, but she hadn't been able to keep up the pace. Leery threw back his head and howled, wincing as all the dogs in the neighborhood answered in kind, then switched to barking madly. He flung himself up the steps, lowering his shoulder and ducking his head as he slammed into the oak door at their summit. The door that could withstand a charging werewolf hadn't been invented yet, and the oak panels split and splintered as they shattered.

The house smelled of sex and its fluidic components, and Leery wrinkled the skin over his snout. The place mimicked Deli's brownstone—white everywhere, punctuated with splotches of color.

Her scent trail went upstairs, so Leery bounded up them on all fours, allowing the low rumble of a growl to burble in the back of his throat.

It never hurt to add a little atmosphere to the chase.

II

A block away, Leery howled, setting off a cacophonous orchestra of canine howls and barks. She sketched a rune designed to let her see despite the darkness, but there was nothing to see. At the end of the alley, a street and another alley waited, but she could detect no movement in either.

His howl must have been for me, she thought. *It came from the right.*

Dru skidded out onto the sidewalk, her eyes scanning both sides of the street. Halfway down the block, the debris of an oak door still clattered down the stoop.

Setting her jaw and sketching another rune set as she ran, Dru dashed across the street and up the steps.

12

Though the darkness almost blinded even his canine vision, Leery didn't slow at the top of the stairs. Deli was close, and the thickness of her scent spoke directly to the wolf part of his brain. His lips wrinkled back from his long fangs, and his ears settled back against his skull. The low rumble in his chest blossomed like an operatic crescendo into the full snarl designed to freeze his prey in its tracks.

In this case, instead of freezing, Delilah Lara opened fire.

13

Dru slipped through the smashed front door and stepped to the right, ears and eyes straining to make sense out of the dark first floor. The scrabbling of Leery's passage at the top of the stairs drew her gaze. His snarl sent shivers of instinctive fear racing down her spine, but she'd been prepared for it by countless Claws at the academy. Instead of going tharn, she raced up the stairs, finishing up the runes to freeze Delilah Lara to the floor.

Chances were that Leery would have Deli down and in custody, but it never hurt to be prepared.

As she neared the second floor, a shotgun blast killed the relative silence.

14

Shotgun pellets slammed into Leery's torso, bringing him up from his running crouch and, if not for his momentum, would have hurled him to a stop. He had nothing to fear from lead pellets, but as he glanced down to assess the damage, he caught sight of a neon red glow surrounding him.

Dru's ward. See that? I told you she was on our side. The only answer his body gave was a low, rumbling growl.

Deli crouched behind the only furniture in the room—a bed, no big surprise there. Leery straightened and pointed a long, claw-tipped finger at her, then shook it back and forth. She grimaced and worked the slide of the pump-action scattergun.

Leery snarled and leaped, clearing the bed in one bound. He landed astride her and batted the shotgun away. He leaned close and growled in her face.

"Yeah, yeah," she said. "Big tough wolf. Look at me, shaking with fear."

It was pure bravado, and he knew it without having to think—her fear-stink filled his nostrils, urging him to clamp his jaws around her puny neck.

Instead, he planted one hand on her chest and pointed at her face with the other. She changed beneath him, becoming the shimmering essence of wolfish femininity, sparking an instinct deep in the animal part of his brain.

His snarl weakened in vigor, almost sounding playful. She writhed beneath him, thrusting her hips and sliding until his hand brushed her breasts. Deli yowled and yipped, speaking in the secret language of his wolf heart, inviting him to take her, to mate, to breed.

Get a hold of yourself, he muttered in his mind, but his wolf side wasn't listening to his human voice. *Has it been that long? You've got to have the first bitch in heat you meet?*

His next growl was directed at himself, and still writhing beneath him, the succubus smiled.

15

Dru slipped on the carpet runner at the top of the stairs and went down hard, slamming her hip into the newel post for good measure. With a grunt, she rolled to her stomach and pushed herself to her feet.

Her ward of protection should have handled the shotgun blast. The sounds coming from the bedroom at the end of the hall worried her more.

She sprinted into the room, eyes straining against the dark. *You'd think a seven-foot-tall wolf wouldn't be hard to see*, she thought with a grimace. She cast about with her hands, searching for a light switch.

16

Leery fought—more with himself than with the writhing she-demon beneath him. He struggled to rein in his wolf, to keep what shreds of control he had left. *Think of your Mitzvah buddies! This could earn you a herem, you stupid pup.*

Even so, he growled to keep himself from voicing the mating call that demanded expression. Deli writhed back and forth, rubbing the wolf-like fur covering her lower stomach against the backs of his thighs, sliding her breasts against his paw.

The worst part, though, was the scent of her desire. The welcoming odor of heat, of invitation, of the promise of sex and a litter of pups. His eyes dilated with the power of it, and his human half despaired.

Listen to me! You think this is a wolf lying beneath you? It isn't, and you know better! Anyway, I'm supposed to be the debauched one between the two of us!

He leaned down toward her, sniffing the elusive scent of her hot pulse in the arteries of her neck, and the musky scent of her fur. Deli lifted her snout, tilting her head back and exposing her throat to his fangs—the ultimate wolf surrender.

A shiver ran through him, and his tongue lolled out of his mouth as he panted to shed the heat rising within him. He leaned closer and licked that path of her carotid artery from the place where her clavicles came together to behind her jaw on the left side of her face.

Get a hold of yourself! Think! Let's talk tachlis, *Lassie. Ever hear of Lilith? You might as well be licking her neck!*

Then the lights flared around him.

"Leery! No!"

Oh, great job, Rin Tin Tin. Now, she'll think we're sex nuts.

A growl rumbled deep in his chest, and he had to fight the urge to turn on this intruder, this usurper. The instinct was strong, despite her female scent, despite knowing she was on his side. Despite his animal urges, he leaned away from Deli, refuting her illusion.

"Down boy," she said and hurled the ward of restraint over the writhing form beneath him. Then she sketched another set of runes in the air, its greenish light momentarily washing out the incandescent bulbs in the overhead light. She flicked the spell at him.

The wolf in him growled as the ward settled over him, his lips curled back, and the skin across the top of his snout wrinkled. Moving stiff-legged, he crawled off his mate and moved between her and Dru's unwanted interference. But even as he did so, her ward began to do its work.

He straightened a little and glanced back at Delilah Lara. *Not a wolf*, he thought. *No fur, no snout, no...no tail—just a manipulative demon, like I said.* Deli's skin was the bleached white of a fish, and her eyes were blood-red from corner to corner. Her ebony hair appeared unwashed, and her mouth was set in a disappointed sneer. A shudder ran through him as he thought of how close a call it had been.

Leery glanced at his partner. She wore runed armor of black leather, her staff collapsed and slung across her back. The gem set into the top of her staff glowed the same neon red that had flashed around him as her ward deflected Lara's shotgun blast, highlighting her dusky, olive-toned skin, and eyes as red as Deli's.

Her true form was just as beautiful as any he'd seen her wear, and he wondered why she bothered playing dress-up.

"You come between me and my dinner, sister," said Deli Lara in a voice like molten sex.

"I'm not your sister, bitch," said Dru. "And that wolf is my Claw. Delilah Lara, you're under arrest on suspicion of murder."

Deli laughed, but Leery could smell the sudden swell of her terror.

Dru glanced at him and hooked her thumb toward the hall. "You have the right to remain silent and to ward yourself from psychic interrogation," she said to Lara. "Anything you say or think during unwarded conversation can be used against you in a court of law. You have the right to representation by a magister of your choosing. If you cannot afford a magister, one will be provided at no cost to you. Do you understand these rights as I've explained them?"

"Get fucked, you little bitch," snarled the succubus. "Your mother would be ashamed of you."

"No doubt. She always has been." She crossed the room in three furious strides. "On your face, little miss thing." She twitched the fingers of her left hand, and Lara spun face down, her hands snapping behind her back.

From where he leaned against the wall, Leery panted and began to regain his human form.

"You and I need to talk, Leery," said Dru. "And then you need to have the same talk with that wolf of yours. I thought he was going to attack me back at the car."

"Yeah, but I didn't let him."

"Still. How am I supposed to work with that?"

"Hey, I kept him off you, didn't I? He's sensitive, that's all. He doesn't like demons *or* vampires."

"Well, that's just tough, because he's partnered with someone who has a little of each in her DNA. I don't care how you have to do it, but get it through his skull that I'm on your side—no matter what skin you're wearing."

"Have you ever argued with a wolf? It's not as easy as all that."

17

A grin stretched the width of Leery's face. "You should have seen it, Lieu. She was a solid pro back there."

"Don't sell me a dog, Leery." Van Helsing looked up at him with bland eyes and a slack expression.

"I have no idea what that means, Lieu. I was born in this century, not when Queen Victoria ruled the roost. Anyway, she sure saved this old carcass. *Twice.*" He gazed through the one-way glass, his eyes following Dru as she circled Delilah Lara's chair. "A real pro. She warded me right from the start. I never asked or anything."

"Oh, so she can do the bare minimum expected of her?" She raised her eyebrows in mock awe. "I'm impressed."

"Come on, Epatha," said Leery with a weary sigh. "She did good."

Van Helsing turned a dead glare on him. "*This* time." She pointed at the interrogation room. "Now, tie your tie and get your ass in there before the skilamalink tart screws the pooch."

Leery wagged his head in his trademark head-shrug and flipped his tie around his neck. The shirt *itched*, but he was used to that—it always did after he let his beast out. Tie tied, he scrubbed his hands through his unruly hair, noting the course, thick quality of it. "I've got the cure for male pattern baldness, Lieu. All it takes is the bite of a werewolf."

"Yeah, yeah."

He tossed Van Helsing an irreverent wink and walked into the interrogation room. "Hello, ladies. What'd I miss?"

Dru scoffed and paced around the table, giving Leery the chair.

Delilah Lara glanced at him. "You're sexier in your wolf skin."

"Oh, I'm hurt," Leery quipped.

She quirked her eyebrow. "Is that your kink? You want me to hurt you, baby?" she crooned.

Without breaking her stride, Dru kicked the back leg of Deli's chair. "Cut it out."

"Or what?"

"Ladies, ladies! There's no need to fight. Plenty of old Leery to go around."

Deli licked her lips, and Dru rolled her eyes.

"Hey, I may be old, but I've got a real wild side."

"Yes," said Delilah in a disinterested monotone.

"Funny!" snapped Dru at the same time.

"And so does Deli, by all accounts. Want to tell us about this kid?" Leery slapped one of the autopsy photos on the table.

Deli leaned forward and peered at the photo. "Never seen him."

"We *know* you did more than look at him, Deli. Your friends at The Red Door told us all about it."

She turned the same disinterested gaze on him she hit him with before. "Lies. Lies told by *meat*."

"Remember Eugenia?" asked Dru. She walked to the foot of the table and leaned against it, looming over Deli. "She's not '*meat*,' is she?"

"Can I smoke?" Ignoring Dru, she looked Leery in the eye. "It'd make me more comfortable."

Dru slapped her hand on the table in front of the succubus. "No, you can't smoke!"

"Come on, Dru. What can it hurt? It isn't as if we'll get cancer."

"Can't you see what's she's doing, Oriscoe? It's that bedroom all over again."

Deli leaned forward and smiled at Leery. "It *could* be."

"Hey, Dru, how about you get us coffee?"

"I don't know. Can I *trust* you alone with her?"

"Don't be like that, Nogan. We'll be just fine while you're gone." He leaned forward and threw a wink at Deli. "Won't we, Deli?"

"More than fine," she purred.

"Oh my God," grumbled Dru. "I think I'm going to be *sick*."

"Better run off to the ladies' room, then," said Delilah.

"You can grab those coffees on your way back. There's a good girl."

With a snort of disgust, Dru pushed off the table and stomped to the room's only door. "It's on you, Oriscoe."

"Fine, fine. Black, two sugars," said Leery with an air of dismissal.

18

Lieutenant Van Helsing gave Dru a stern look. "You did all right, Nogan. Next time, don't bubble around so much."

"Uh, okay."

"Don't lay the disdain on quite so thick. You want the skell to think Leery's on their side, but you can't make it so obvious."

Dru nodded and turned to watch Leery through the window. "Thanks, Lieu. In this case, that slut and I had already had words that were sharp and pointy. I figured if I backed off, it would put her hairs on end."

Van Helsing looked at her askance. "You've got decent instincts."

"Thanks, Lieu."

In the interrogation room, Leery leaned across the table and put a cigarette between Deli's open lips, then lit it with a cheap plastic lighter. As he sank back, he hesitated, glancing at the mirrored glass. "She won't be gone long."

Deli chuckled. "She's right behind that glass, and you know it.

"Nah," said Leery with a smile. "She doesn't want to watch. Her oath chafes."

Delilah spared a glance at the mirrored glass. "It's disgusting. Why one of my sisters would make an oath of abstinence is beyond me."

"She wanted to be a cop," said Leery with a shrug.

"I don't get that, either, but even so, why wouldn't your bosses want her to *use* her abilities?"

"Prudes. You should see our lieutenant. She's a ghost from the Victorian era." He shook his open hand in front of his torso. "Talk about straitlaced…"

"A ghost?"

"Yeah. She's from the Van Helsing clan to boot."

Deli made a face.

"Just be glad you're not a vampire."

"Or a werewolf." She blew smoke out through the side of her mouth and leaned forward, eyes dancing. "Want to show me your fur?"

"Boy do I, but I can't. Not yet."

Deli smirked and leaned back in her chair. She folded one arm across her chest and cupped her opposite elbow, forearm up, cigarette leaking smoke toward the ceiling. "Fine. I knew him."

"The boy in the picture."

"*Not* a boy, wolfman. You should have seen what he wanted to do." She wagged her eyebrows at him. "Maybe I can show you."

"Maybe. So, what, he wanted more and more? He pushed you, right? If this was an accident, you need to tell me. I can *help* you here, Deli."

"Such as he could never *push* me, Leery. Not like you could. You could push *all* my buttons."

"Later, I promise. This is important. If he attacked you, say, I could get the Assistant Locus Magister to go easy. He's not a prude like these cops."

She chuckled. "Oh, wolfie... Eddie was a kink, but he'd never attack me. He left my arms satisfied and worn-out." She leaned forward and stabbed her cigarette toward Leery. "But the point is, *he left my arms.*"

"Alive?"

She smirked and made a shooing motion with the two fingers holding the cigarette.

"That was clumsy, lover. But, yes. He left me on his own two feet, upright and breathing."

Leery cocked his head to the side and looked down at the folder in his lap. "Hmm. It says here he died having sex."

The lopsided smirk alit on Deli's lips once more. "You can't know that. It's impossible."

"Come on, Deli. Haven't you heard about our CSI team?"

"Crime-scene…"

"Conjuration, Scrying, and Invocation. They speak to the dead, Deli. Dead like poor Eddie, here."

Deli's left eye twitched, but her smirk didn't fade. "Tell him 'hello' for me. But if your spooks really spoke to him, then you know I didn't do anything but give him the best night of his life—past, present, *and* future." She tilted her head to the side and grinned. "Do you want this night to be the best of your life?"

"If you only knew how many of my ex-wives promised the same thing…"

"Were any of them succubi?"

"Well, no."

Deli nodded and waved her cigarette, as if to say, "there you go."

"I guess the point is that Eddie *didn't* tell us any such thing."

Deli shrugged one delicate shoulder. "Lies."

"Back to that? Come on, sugar. Tell me what happened so I can figure a way out of this for you."

"After we've been together, you will do this for me, anyway. And without any preconditions that I tell you anything." She slid out of the chair with a dancer's grace and began to unbutton the black button-down shirt she wore. She winked at him. "Want me to do yours too?"

The door banged open, and Dru stood on the threshold, holding three steaming mugs. "What did I miss, ladies?"

"Everything your mother tried to teach you," snarled Deli, thumping down in the chair. She glanced at Leery. "Later, lover."

"You know it." Leery took the cup Dru offered him and set it on the table without looking at it. "You picked a fine time to come back."

Dru dimpled and pretended to curtesy. "I live to please." She turned a hostile gaze on Deli. "Did this skank tell you she murdered him, yet?"

Delilah rolled her eyes. "No, I told him the truth. Eddie left my place satisfied *and* drawing breath." She waved her cigarette at the ceiling. "Breathing hard, maybe, but breathing."

"Come on, Lara! Smarten up! We've got you cold!" snapped Leery.

Deli smirked at him. "No more lovey-lover talk, Leery?"

Dru held up her hand and ticked the charges off on her fingers, one by one. "Attempted magical seduction of a law enforcement officer, attempted sexual assault one, attempted murder—"

"Who did I try to kill?" Deli demanded.

"Uh, this guy?" said Leery, hooking both thumbs at his chest.

"Very funny," Dru said and scowled at him.

"A guy's gotta have jokes for times like this."

"Hate to break it to you, sweet cheeks. That one's a werewolf. I could no more kill him with a shotgun than I could turn him into a marshmallow sculpture of Gandhi."

"Now, there's a mental image," murmured Leery.

"You didn't know he was a werewolf when you pulled out that shotgun."

"Didn't I? Can you *prove* that?"

Dru shrugged. "Intent follows the bullet."

"Spoken like a magister."

Dru snatched the cigarette out of Deli's hand and stubbed it out on the corner of the table. She dropped the extinguished butt into Deli's coffee. "Haven't you heard of CSI, Lara?"

Deli laughed and waved her hand at Leery.

"Deli's not a believer," he said. "She insists on this silly story that Eddie just wanted sex, and she was happy to give it to him."

Dru chuckled. "You told her we know Eddie died mid-coitus?"

"Oh, such big words," snapped Deli.

"I did."

"Have you told her we were just waiting on the Magical Examiner's report? That they detected fluids on the body?"

Deli narrowed her eyes and drew her lips into a thin line. "I've already admitted we had sex."

"Digestive juices, it says here." Dru pulled a folded piece of paper out of her pocket. "Here's the email version, Leery. I know you don't play well with computers."

"That's not a thing!"

"Oh, it's a thing," said Dru. "You see, I didn't block out *everything* my mother taught me."

Delilah cast her gaze down at her lap, but not before both cops saw her biting her lip. "So much science, these days," she muttered.

"An old girl like you must find it hard to keep up," said Dru with a malicious grin.

Leery put the blank piece of paper in the folder of blank printer paper he held in his lap. "That spells trouble for you, Ms. Lara."

She mumbled something that Dru couldn't hear, but Leery flashed a satisfied grin at Dru.

"What?"

"She just said, 'I never should have drained him all the way.'"

Deli raised her head, her gaze snapping with anger. "Werewolves!" she snarled.

Leery smiled and spread his arms wide. "Don't you just love us?"

The succubus snarled and looked away.

"Come on, Deli," said Dru. "You've already admitted it. Do yourself some good here."

"How?" she asked in a sullen, barely audible voice.

"Write up what happened," said Leery, sliding a pen and a blank piece of paper across the table. "I'll go to bat with Sam McCoy myself if it comes to that. We'll shoot for a reduced sentence."

"Fine!" Deli snapped as she picked up the pen.

19

L eery and Dru followed the uniformed cop leading Deli away in handcuffs out of the interrogation room. "Good work, you two," said Lieutenant Van Helsing.

"What did you get?" asked Angie Carmichael, the ALM assigned to the Supernatural Inquisition bureau.

Leery presented Lara's signed confession with a flourish. "Everything's all here." Leery thought she was a knockout—olive skin, jet black hair, the figure of a supermodel, and a powerful witch to boot.

Angie scanned the single sheet of paper, grimacing at the spelling and grammar, then nodded. "Hook her up." She nodded to Van Helsing. "Good work, Epatha."

"All I did was stand here. Leery did the heavy lifting."

Angie nodded and walked to the exit door. "Good work. This case is a slam dunk."

As the door closed behind her, Van Helsing turned to her two officers. "Cup of coffee?" she asked, quirking her insubstantial eyebrow at Dru.

Leery grinned. "Can't ever have too much coffee."

"It makes the world go 'round," said Van Helsing. "Not as much as when the Dutch East India Company ran everything, but still." She turned and walked toward the door. "Come on. I'll spring for the swill they call coffee in the shop across the street." She turned and floated toward the door.

"Uh, I—"

"She'll be happy to, Lieu," said Leery. He leaned close to her ear and whispered, "You don't have to drink it." He pushed Dru firmly after Van Helsing.

Van Helsing nodded. "You didn't screw anything up, Nogan."

Dru kept her eyes pointed at the floor. "Thanks."

"And you showed good instincts. Maybe I won't have to knock you down to uniform."

"Thanks," Dru repeated.

"You two worked well together. What do you say, Leery?"

"I'm happy, Lieu."

"Fine, then." Van Helsing disappeared and reappeared facing them while floating backward toward the elevator. "Let's make it official. You two are partners henceforth." Without waiting for a reply, she disappeared and reappeared facing the elevator.

Dru glanced at Leery and raised her eyebrows. "I thought we were already partners," she hissed.

"Yeah. We are. Were. Now, it's just permanent." He patted her shoulder. "You done good, kid."

"Don't call me that," Dru said absently. Her gaze had attached to Van Helsing's translucent back. She glanced at Leery and raised a warding hand. "That backward thing is creepy, isn't it?"

Leery grimaced.

"I'm a ghost, harlot. I see in a three-hundred-sixty-degree arc without the need of eyes."

Dru made a face.

"But, to answer your question, it *is* creepy. That's why I did it."

CHAPTER 3

THE TRIAL

I

Executive Assistant Locus Magister Sam McCoy grimaced and looked up from his work. "Well? Is the case a dog, or isn't it?"

"Not," said Angie. "We had a confession before the ME report came in, and we have solid spectral evidence, though the victim is too traumatized by his death to do much more than wail and carry-on." She grimaced. "I hate the Irish."

Sam lifted an eyebrow. "Present company excepted, I hope?"

"Most of the time," said Angie with a flirty grin.

"I'll keep that in mind during annual reviews." He grinned a moment longer, then turned and sat behind his desk. "Tell me about this Lara woman."

"She's a succubus, not a woman."

"The difference being?"

"The word 'woman' denotes a human being."

"To you, maybe. I'm not sure it is defined in the Canon and Covenants as anything other than female. Are ghosts no longer women? But never mind." Sam waved it away and wagged his craggy eyebrows. "You know, they say once you've gone demon—"

"Then you're dead. *That's* what they say."

McCoy laughed. "I guess that's right."

"I don't see the attraction, Sam—it's like an obsession to kiss a moving freight train. Do I have to worry about you during this trial?"

"No, it's the *jurors* that should worry you."

Angie nodded. "Yeah, don't remind me."

"All it takes is one smitten idiot..."

"Or one smitten ALM."

"Don't worry about me. I've sworn off females—demons included."

2

The next morning, Angie stood before Magistrate Harry Houdini—or the ghost of Harry Houdini, at any rate. Delilah Lara stood by the defense table, dressed in a tailored linen suit, hair brushed slick and back from her face. Beside her stood Tovah

Melnick, one of the best defense magisters working in the Locus of New York.

Houdini grimaced as the gavel slipped through his hand. With an angry grunt, he concentrated long enough to bang the gavel. "And what have I done to deserve a visit from not the one, not the two, but the *three* lovely examples of feminine grace I see standing before me?" He cut his gaze away from them and glared at his undead clerk.

"Docket number 1421981, The People versus Delilah Lara."

"What's the charge?"

"Magical murder in the first degree," said Angie.

"Bail application?" Houdini arched an eyebrow at the defense table. "Ms. Melnick?"

"We'd like a release on her own recognizance, Your Honor. My client was pressured into giving a false confession under duress—"

"There's a laugh," said Angie. "We have spectral evidence, Judge, as well as physical evidence at the crime scene and on the body."

"My client freely admits to having consensual sex with the victim, Your Honor. But she didn't murder anyone."

"No, she consumed his essence as a snack."

"As much as I enjoy seeing you two wrangle, save it for the trial judge." He glanced at Lara. "Succubus, huh? Enjoy your stay at Rikers." He glared at the gavel, then shifted his gaze at his clerk. She lifted a duplicate and banged it on her desk.

Melnick followed Angie into the corridor. "Kind of a rush to judgment on this one."

"Hardly. Does the phrase 'slam dunk' mean anything to you?"

"Sure, but they're pretty rare in a magical court. Tell Sam I want a meeting."

"We're not cutting a deal on this one."

"Just tell him." She stepped away, but then turned back and threw Angie a wink. "And don't bet your soul on not accepting a deal. Sam is usually more circumspect than he has been in this case."

3

S am arched an eyebrow that had more in common with a porcupine than a human eyebrow as Angie relayed the message. "What does Tovah have?" he asked. "She doesn't ask for a meeting unless she's got an ace up her sleeve."

Angie lifted her shoulders and let them drop. "Dunno, Sam. She didn't say, but she made a crack about you being more circumspect than this."

Sam twitched his head to the side. "Well, I guess we'll find out what cards she holds." He inclined his head and glanced at Angie out of the corner of his eye. "You're still sure about this case? There's nothing you're holding back?"

"Not a thing, Sam. And this case is a slam dunk, I don't care what Melnick says."

"Speak of the devil, and he shall appear," said Melnick from the open doorway. She whirled into Sam's office, followed by Delilah Lara, who wore handcuffs inscribed with numerous runes, including a prohibition of seductive charm.

"Welcome," said Sam. "Have a seat, ladies."

"Though this won't be a long meeting," grumbled Angie as she slid into a seat across from Tovah and Delilah.

"Well, now," said Melnick. "I doubt that. Not when you two hear what I have to say."

Sam shrugged and sat behind his desk. "It's your ten minutes, Tovah."

"Sam, you've got this case wrong. Yes, my client is a succubus. Yes, she's a sex worker. Yes, she feeds on the sexual gratification of her clients." Tovah glanced at Angie. "Where's the harm in that?"

"So far, you haven't told us anything we don't already know." Angie crossed her arms under her breasts.

"That may be," said Tovah with a secretive smile. "But that doesn't mean I don't know things you don't know."

"Like what?" asked Sam, leaning forward and steepling his fingers in front of his face.

"That would ruin the surprise." Tovah wrinkled the skin on her nose and grinned.

"We wouldn't want that."

"No. But I'll tell you this, Sam: if you take this to trial, you'll lose."

Sam smiled and sat back in his chair. "Empty bravado doesn't win cases, Tovah."

"You know me better than that, Sam."

His smile faded. "I'm supposed to take Ms. Lara at her word that she's innocent?"

Tovah leaned back and put one elbow on the back of her chair, looking smug and happy. "I didn't say that. Let's just say that this case is woven out of reasonable doubt."

Angie snorted. "Sam, this is a waste of time."

He glanced at her and said nothing for the space of a breath. "No, we'll hear Tovah out."

"Thank you, Sam."

"You have to tell me enough to make me believe you, Tovah. Evidence?"

"Not without a deal on the table."

Sam scoffed. "A deal? Based on what you've said? Okay, here's my offer: one lifetime in a warded dungeon."

"Come on, Sam. You can't be serious."

Sam glanced at Angie. "Angie says this is a slam dunk and shows me buckets full of evidence. You say it's a loser but won't say why, let alone show me actual evidence. You can't possibly believe your position warrants a plea deal."

"It does." She tossed a wink at Angie and shrugged.

A wry smile bloomed on Sam's face. "Then prove it."

"No, Sam. When I do that, it will be in a courtroom."

He chuckled and spread his hands. "Then we should continue this talk there."

"In front of a judge and jury," Melnick added.

"That's fine with me, Tovah. But don't expect kid gloves."

"I wouldn't dream of it, Sam. Come on, Delilah." The two stood and walked to the door, where Melnick paused. "I'm going to enjoy this, Sam."

"You've held that grudge since I kicked your ass in moot court, Tovah. It's time to let it go."

"We'll see, Sam." Her face morphed into a smiling, predatory expression. "We'll see."

After they'd gone, Sam crossed to the door and closed it firmly. He turned to Angie and frowned. "We're in trouble."

"No, we're not, Sam. Don't let her rattle you."

Shaking his head, he said, "You don't know Tovah like I do. She doesn't bluff, and she's been nursing that grudge for twenty years. If she hadn't made the crack about enjoying it, I might shrug it all off." He crossed to stand next to her chair, and she turned to face him. "You'd better go through the case file again." He went to his desk, ignoring her pronounced sigh. "And call Oriscoe. Have him check all his little duckies."

"You're the boss, Sam," said Angie through a grimace.

"That's right, I am." He let Angie get to the door, then said, "I don't want to lose this, Angie. Not to Tovah."

"Why don't you two just spend the night together and get over it?"

Sam's eyes twinkled as he laughed. "That would ruin the surprise," he said.

"After twenty years, the surprise might not be good."

He sobered and turned his gaze to the stack of files on his desk. "Go make sure the case is as solid as you think."

4

Leery frowned and scrubbed the hand not holding his phone through his hair. "But it's solid, Angie." Dru arched an eyebrow at him, but he waved her off. "No, there's no other suspect. Evidently, she's the only one who would take the kid's money. The only succubus, anyway." He listened for a moment longer, then grimaced. "Well, thanks for sharing the pain. We'll go over it again, but I've got to tell Epatha, so you'd better authorize the overtime." He set the phone back in the cradle with care then slumped back in his chair. "You'll never guess who that was."

"Angie Carmichael, and she wants us to retrace our steps."

Leery flashed her a crooked smile. "You must be a detective." He stretched and stood. "Come on. You might as well learn how to get screamed at by the lieutenant."

With an uncertain expression, Dru got up and followed him into Van Helsing's office.

5

Two days later, Dru, Leery, and Angie entered Sam's office together and stood in an array on the other side of his desk. He was in the middle of scribbling notes illegibly in the margin of a draft motion and held up one finger. When he finished, he looked at them each in turn. "Well?" he asked when he'd finished.

"Nothing, Sam."

"There's got to be something. Tovah doesn't bluff. I told you that."

"Yeah, well, in this case, she must be."

"My second ex-wife spent ten years purposefully not bluffing so I'd believe she was a straight-shooter," said Leery. "She let me know how wrong I was in the divorce."

Sam grinned. "You, too?"

"Yeah. But with regard to Delilah Lara, there's nothing there. She did it, and she admitted as much."

Sam sat back in his chair and looked at them over steepled fingers. "You've been through it all? Retraced your steps?"

"Yeah," Angie and Dru said in unison.

"Leery?"

Leery lifted one hand and let it drop. "We re-interviewed all the witnesses, reviewed the forensics with the magical examiner. Hell, we even endured a meeting with the spooks from CSI. If there's something we missed, I can't see it."

"Then we move forward," said Sam.

"You'll get her, counselor," said Leery. "They don't call you the Stakeman for nothing."

Sam grimaced. "I don't like that nickname."

"That doesn't mean it isn't accurate," said Leery with a good-natured grin.

6

The courtroom was half-full when Sam arrived carrying a box of notes and reports. Angie was already seated at the prosecution table, but Tovah Melnick and Delilah Lara were nowhere to be seen.

"Good morning, Sam," said Angie.

"What's good about it? I didn't sleep a wink imagining all the tricks Tovah might pull."

"Relax, boss. We've got a slam dunk, like I've always said."

"Well, we're about to find out," Sam said, watching Tovah enter from the hall, an enormous grin on her face. She met Sam's gaze and tossed a wink in his direction. He turned away and frowned down at the box he still held in his hands. "We're in trouble."

"Slam dunk, remember?"

"You don't know Tovah like I do. She's never this happy unless she knows her hammer is bigger than yours. I'm telling you, Angie, we're in trouble, and we'd better figure it out before the iron jaws of her trap spring closed on our necks."

"Sam—"

"Angie! Do as I bid you!"

"Fine, fine." She treated him to sullen stare for the space of a breath. "I'll go call Oriscoe again, but I'm telling you, there's nothing to worry about."

"Oh, there is, Angie," said Sam, ducking his head to watch Tovah Melnick advance through the gallery, a wide smirk stretching her lips.

"Hello, Sam," she said.

"Tovah."

Angie stood and edged past Melnick. "Excuse me a moment," she muttered.

"Going to call Oriscoe?" asked Tovah with a wink at Sam.

Angie shook her head and left them.

Sam put the box down on the prosecution table and stood leaning over it for a moment. "Ready to tell me, yet?" he asked without looking at her.

"Tell you? No, I'm not going to just tell *you*, Sam."

"What is it, Tovah? What do you have?"

"That would be telling, and where's the fun in that?" Her grin expanded, and she patted his bicep. "You'll find out, though. I promise you that."

"That's what scares me, Tovah."

She cocked her head to the side and looked at him while the massive clock on the wall behind the jury box ticked away for twenty seconds. "I'll tell you right now, Sam. All you have to do is make me a deal."

"You mean, make Delilah Lara a sweetheart deal." He stretched his lips in a tight, wide line, shaking his head. "She's no sweetheart, Tovah. She's *dangerous*."

"That she is, Sam. Wouldn't it be better to put her behind bars for *any* amount of time than *none* at all?"

"What you have is that strong?" He asked the question at a volume just above that of a whisper.

"Yes."

"Give me a hint, Tovah. For old time's sake." As soon as he said it, Sam knew he'd made a grievous tactical mistake.

Melnick's grin widened, and a predatory gleam entered her eyes. "For old time's sake? Sam, I'm giving you the chance to make a deal for that very reason." She ducked her chin to look at him from beneath her brows. "Proceed at your own risk." Then she winked at him and whirled away to begin organizing her materials on the defense table.

7

Shaking his head, Leery said, "What can I tell you, Lieu? McCoy's paranoid." He slumped into the Van Helsing's guest chair and glanced at Nogan for support.

Van Helsing floated out of her chair, drifting toward the ceiling—a sure sign she was upset. "Twice, Leery! Twice, the LM's office has ordered you to look at this again. Is there *any* possibility that Delilah Lara didn't do this?"

"None," said Dru.

Epatha Van Helsing raised a spectral hand like a traffic cop of a foregone age, ordering her to shut up without looking at her. "Leery?"

Oriscoe stood staring off into space.

"What? What is it, Leery?" Van Helsing drifted closer to him, a sepulchral chill emanating from her in waves.

He grunted. "Maybe it's too neat, Lieu."

She lifted her chin and narrowed her eyes. "Explain."

"It was too easy. Like we followed the breadcrumbs right into the witch's house instead of back to safety."

"Come on, Oriscoe," muttered Dru. "We followed the *evidence* right to Lara's door. She did it. Even she says so. We *know* she did."

"Is that right?" asked Epatha with deceptive mildness. "How do you know?"

Leery thought about giving his partner a warning look, but she had to learn somehow. What's coming might be painful, but painful lessons were often the best. "Do tell, Dru," he said.

Nogan bobbed her head and began ticking the points off her fingers. "Eddie Thompson was easily identified—he had his wallet in his pocket. His name led us to Fiona Rae Gill, the Irish Ambassador to the United Nations. Ms. Gill not only confirmed the identification but instructed her underling to cooperate fully. She's Thompson's next of kin here in the States. Her secretary admitted to taking Eddie on several romps through the seedier sex clubs in Times Square. At a dump called The Red Door, we talked to the club owner, and he remembered seeing Eddie leave the club in Delilah Lara's company. We surveilled Lara after unsuccessfully trying to interview her in her brownstone. She took off, and we chased her. She used every trick she knew to seduce

Leery, to get him to let her go and probably"—she cut her gaze away from the lieu, brushing Oriscoe's gaze for a moment—"to consume his essence, boosting her power. During the interview, she confessed to killing Thompson." Dru shrugged. "*Quod erat demonstradum.*"

"And you see nothing in that chain of events that might seem weird? No unexplored avenues?"

Dru pressed her lips into a thin line, shaking her head.

Van Helsing drifted toward the ceiling; eyes closed. When she opened them, they blazed down at Oriscoe. "Is she too pretty?" she demanded.

Leery had been watching Nogan. He'd wanted to see how she reacted to the tongue-lashing he was sure would follow. "What, Lieu?" he asked. His stomach sank toward the floor as he met Van Helsing's gaze and saw the red-hot anger there. "Is who too pretty?"

Epatha twitched her head toward Nogan. "Your partner. Your partner, the succubus. Is she too pretty?"

"I don't get it, Lieu."

"Has she seduced you?"

"I've done nothing—"

Van Helsing froze Nogan with a look, then turned her gaze back on Oriscoe, quirking one eyebrow.

"No, Lieu. She's been the perfect gentleman."

"Cute!" snapped Van Helsing. "But that doesn't explain how you allowed this train wreck to happen."

"Train wreck, Lieu? That hardly seems fair. I mean—"

"Don't you see it, Oriscoe? Even now? *Someone* led you by the nose, right to Lara. Why would they do that?" Van Helsing's gaze flitted away to impale Nogan. "Someone wanted this solved quickly. Someone wanted a lone succubus to be found and prosecuted. Maybe someone wanted to protect a loved one." She drifted toward Nogan, still floating up near the ceiling, forcing both detectives to look up at her as though they were errant children. "Like a mother. Or a father."

"Lieu—" Van Helsing twitched her index finger at him, and Oriscoe bit back his words with a shake of his head.

"Someone with ties to a particular community of people who can't be trusted. Someone with charms all her own."

Dru's eyes narrowed, and her face blazed brick-red. Her nostrils flared but said nothing—wisely.

"Lieu, trust me," said Oriscoe. "You're way off base."

"Am I, Leery? *Am I?*"

"Yes, Lieu. You didn't see Dru in the field. You didn't see her face as she worked the evidence, as she interviewed other succubi, as she stood up to their bully tactics and derisions."

Van Helsing's ethereal form flickered with agitation. "That's *exactly* what I'd expect an enthralled man to say."

"Come on, Lieu. You know me better than that."

The lieutenant dismissed his argument with a hard glance, then turned back to Dru. "And you, slattern? What have you to say in your defense?"

"In my defense?" echoed Dru. "What do *you* say in your defense? Or should we leave that for the review board?" Her voice was mild, but

Oriscoe had the definite feeling that rage ran rampant in her veins.

"My defense, quean? Why do I need a defense? And a review board?" Van Helsing rolled her ghostly eyes, but her substance seemed to flicker, and Leery knew Dru had struck a nerve.

"Listen, both of you are—"

"Shut up, Oriscoe," said both his partner and his lieutenant in perfect unison.

"I'll tell you something, Van Helsing. I've spent—"

"Please do."

"—my *entire* life dealing with bigots. If you think—"

"Bigots? *Bigots?*" Van Helsing's form flickered in and out of existence like a light bulb losing its shit.

"—you're the first, you're sadly mistaken. I've been discriminated against by the best minds in the New York Locus. If you believe one more diatribe against *my kind* is going to upset me, to...to...to drive me away, you've got another thing coming."

The very air seemed to crackle with emotion, but neither woman spoke. Leery plastered a smile on his face. "Hey, that was a great song, right?" He cleared his throat and sang. "Dunh-dunh-dunhdah-dunh-dunh-dunh-dunh-dunh. One life, I'm gonna live it up..."

"Get out, Oriscoe," hissed Van Helsing.

"Come on, Lieutenant. This is going—"

"Out!"

Leery grimaced and threw a sympathetic glance at Nogan, then lifted his shoulders in a helpless shrug. "Right, boss. I'll be at my desk waiting for my partner."

"You do that, Oriscoe," said Van Helsing in a voice as cold as death. "This darling little chippie and I are going to have a little chat."

Blowing out a deep breath, Leery turned and left the office, closing the door behind him. As he made his way to his desk, Dru and Epatha's voices rose to screaming volume. The other detectives in the squad glanced at the lieutenant's office, then at Oriscoe. "What? You've never heard a cat fight before today? Mind your business." He slumped into his chair. *Should have managed that better. Now, I'll probably have to break in a new partner or maybe a new lieutenant...and they're much harder to train. Hell, maybe they'll make me the lieutenant. Then we're all fucked.*

To distract himself from the screaming acrimony echoing through the squad room, Leery flipped open the Eddie Thompson murder book and began flipping through it, starting with the first page. His gaze scanned quickly through the pages, then paused and went back a page to reread it. "I'll be damned," he muttered, rereading Dru's notes of the interview with the Irish Ambassador. After he'd read it three times, he leaped to his feet and ran back into Van Helsing's office, bursting in as the screaming reached a fevered pitch. "Hate to interrupt—"

"Shut up and get out, Oriscoe! I'll let you know when I want to hear from you again."

"Oh, you want to hear from me right now, Lieu. Believe me." When she turned narrowed eyes on him and stared daggers into his heart, he gestured for her to wait. "I know what we missed."

As if he'd thrown a switch, Van Helsing went from full, murderous rage to icy calm. "Tell me."

And he did.

8

When the bailiff stepped to the front of the room, Angie still hadn't returned. Sam darted a glance over his shoulder, hoping to see the gallery doors swinging open, but they remained stubbornly closed.

"Hear ye, hear ye! Please rise. The Magical Court of the First Locus, Criminal Division, is now in session, the Honorable Judge Aleister Crowley presiding."

Crowley appeared out of the ether next to his seat up on the bench. "Be seated," he said. "Bailiff Haddo, please swear in the jury."

As Haddo droned the oath to the jury and they all said, "I do," Sam spun around and glared at the gallery door, willing Angie to come through it. Crowley began his instructions to the jury, and still, the doors remained closed.

"Something catch your eye, Mr. McCoy?" asked Crowley.

Sam twisted around to face the court. "No, Your Honor. My apologies."

"Bailiff Haddo, you may continue."

"Your Honor, today's case is the People of the Locus of New York versus Delilah Lara. The charge is magical murder in the first degree."

Crowley gave Sam the stink-eye. "Is the prosecution ready to proceed?"

Sam threw one desperate glance over his shoulder, then nodded. "We are, Judge."

Crowley turned to Tovah Melnick. "And you, Ms. Melnick? Is the defense ready?"

With a mischievous glance at Sam, Tovah said, "More than ready, Your Honor."

"Then we'll move to opening statements. Mr. McCoy?"

"Thank you, Judge Crowley." Sam stood and walked around the table. He fished two boxes the size of his fist out of the larger box he'd brought with him and arrayed them within easy reach. "Your Honor, members of the jury, my name is Sam McCoy, and I represent the People in this proceeding. I intend to prove that the defendant, Delilah Lara by name, did willfully and with significant malice, end the life of Edward Thompson, a tourist from Ireland." Sam opened one of the small boxes and took out a fully fleshed apple.

"Lara committed this act using magical means, to wit, using her powers as a succubus to first charm, then mesmerize the victim as she drained his essence, thus ending his existence in this mortal realm." McCoy opened the other small box and removed a desiccated apple, setting it next to the ripe one.

"While I appreciate the theater, Your Honor, I must object. This melodrama is prejudicial in the extreme, and, entirely irrelevant to these proceedings," said Melnick as she stood. "Further—"

"Overruled, Ms. Melnick."

"But, Your Honor—"

"I've ruled."

"Thank you, Judge," said Melnick, sounding a little put-out.

Sam couldn't help but smile.

"Proceed, Mr. Prosecutor."

"Thank you, Your Honor." He turned his attention back to the jury—which was composed of five witches or warlocks, two zombies, a skin walker, three cloven-hoofed demons, and a day-walking vampire. "Members of the jury, we all know, in essence, what happens to the victims of succubi—at least in principle." He passed the dried apple to the first juror and waved for her to pass it down the line after she'd looked at it. "But Edward Thompson died with a large blind put between him and that knowledge we all take for granted. The blind was placed in his mind by the defendant willfully and with the intent of hiding her actions from the victim. Actions that resulted in him leaving the mortal coil and leaving behind the husk of his body." Sam muttered an incantation, and a life-sized vision of Thompson's mummified remains appeared in front of the jury box.

"Your Honor!" cried Tovah in the indignant half-screech she reserved for the most egregious of courtroom hijinks. "This is going too far!"

"Mr. Prosecutor? I'm inclined to agree with Ms. Melnick."

"Your Honor, by the Canon and Covenants, I'm allowed certain privileges—one of which is the leeway to present the evidence by magical means. I assure Your Honor that this simple illusion is exact in every detail, and I can have the Magical Examiner testify as such."

Crowley turned his gaze back to the magister for the defense. "He's got you, Ms. Melnick. Objection overruled." As Tovah opened her mouth to argue further, he held up an ethereal index finger. "But, Mr. Prosecutor, what's good for the goose can't be allowed to ruin the pudding."

"Uh..." Sam cast about in his mind, trying to figure out what that might mean, but then he gave up and took the safest route out of the quagmire. "Yes, Your Honor. Thank you."

Crowley treated him to a single nod and a benevolent smile. "Good enough, Ms. Melnick?"

Tovah glanced at Sam, just as mystified as he'd been. "Uh...sure. Thank you, Your Honor."

"Very well. Proceed, Mr. McCoy."

Sam muttered another incantation, and the ME's reconstruction of how Thompson had appeared in life stood next to the desiccated version. "This, ladies and gentlemen of the jury, is how Mr. Thompson *should* look." He held his hand over the reconstructed illusion. "And it's how he looked when he purchased the defendant's...er...services." He switched sides, holding his hand over the mummified head of the first illusion. "This, however, is how the defendant left him when she dumped him in Riverside Park less than an hour after taking him to the apartment on the Upper West Side where she plies her trade as a common prostitute. I think you'll join me in my outrage at the defendant's savage actions." He turned to glare at Delilah Lara, who returned his gaze with serenity, if not boredom. "Edward Thompson was nineteen years old, ladies and gentlemen. Imagine that—nineteen short years on this planet, then thrust into the afterlife without so much as a warning. Over the next few days, I will present evidence supporting every detail of my opening statement. At the end of the defense's case, you will, no doubt, return a verdict of guilty, rewarding Delilah Lara with her just deserts." Sam turned and walked around the prosecution table, again glancing at the gallery doors. He'd wanted Angie in court to read the jury for his opening statement and to take notes during Melnick's. With a small sigh, he sat in his seat. "Thank you, ladies and gentlemen, for your attention, and thank you, Your Honor, for the privilege of presenting my opening statement in this august chamber."

"Very well, Mr. Prosecutor." Crowley treated him to a slow nod. "Ms. Melnick? Are you ready to begin your opening statement?"

"Your Honor, I'd like to exercise my right to present my opening statement at the beginning of the defense's case."

Crowley turned his gaze on Sam and arched an eyebrow. "Objections from the prosecution?"

Sam looked at Tovah through narrowed eyelids. After a moment, he shrugged. "None, Your Honor, though I must remark on the irregularity of the request."

"Though you, no doubt, admit its legality?"

"Yes, Judge Crowley."

"Are you ready to proceed, Mr. McCoy?"

Sam glanced at Melnick, then at the gallery doors once more. "If it pleases the court, I'd like to beg Your Honor's indulgence—"

"I've already noted Ms. Carmichael's absence. Most irregular, sir."

"Yes, Your Honor. I sent Ms. Carmichael on an errand crucial to the people's case. May I beg a short recess to find what's keeping her?"

"Very well. This court stands in recess until after lunch." The judge stared at his gavel for a moment, then grasped it and banged it.

9

S am slammed through his office door and set the box of exhibits and papers on the credenza behind his desk. He stabbed the intercom button with his index finger and shouted, "Angie!" into it. When she didn't answer, he muttered to himself and strode across the hall into the cubicle Angie Carmichael shared with another Assistant Locus Magister. When he didn't find her there either, he threw up his hands in disgust and decided to go buy his lunch.

As he approached the elevators, one of them opened to reveal Angie and Lieutenant Van Helsing. "There you are!" he groused.

"I think we found it, Sam. Or Leery Oriscoe did, at any rate."

"So this slam dunk isn't such a slam dunk?"

She avoided his angry eyes. "Let's go into your office, Sam, and we'll explain."

Sam tsked and treated them both to a single shake of his head. "I've already started my case, you know."

"Just hear what we have to say, Sam."

He led them to his office and tromped around behind his desk. "Someone had better start explaining."

Angie nodded her head. "What Melnick has…" She glanced at Van Helsing for support.

"Lara murdered Thompson on her own," said the lieutenant. "She acted in proxy."

"In proxy? Murder for hire?" He glared at Angie. "This 'slam dunk' gets better and better. It's too late to amend the charges, Angie! Jeopardy has attached!"

"I know, Sam. I know."

"Tell me." He turned his hard gaze on Epatha Van Helsing and crossed his arms over his chest. "Explain to me how the brilliant detectives of the Supernatural Inquisitors Squad missed a damn co-conspirator!"

The picture of icy calm, Van Helsing floated a step closer to the Executive Assistant Locus Magister. "They missed it, all right, but there are mitigating circumstances. One of my detectives—this is her first case, and to be honest, she shouldn't even be—"

"I don't want to hear your problems, Lieutenant!" he snapped.

"Fine, McCoy. We missed it—and when I say 'we,' that includes you—because the co-

conspirator *wanted* us to miss it. She worked hard to ensure we all missed it."

"Everyone does! We're supposed to be better than that!"

"Not everyone has the skill and power to cast a geas over veteran members of the department and the Locus Magister's office."

"A geas? There hasn't been a documented case—"

"There is now," said Angie. "The Magical Examiner has confirmed it."

Sam sank into his chair, no longer hungry. In fact, he felt sick to his stomach.

"You can thank Oriscoe for thinking of it. He was rereading a witness statement when it struck him."

"What? When what struck him?"

"The ambassador's receptionist didn't seem to recognize the boy, seemed to have forgotten all about spending nights out with Thompson. It was as if he'd completely forgotten about taking him to sex clubs. He'd forgotten until Fiona Rae Gill was present and told him to speak what he knew."

"Maybe he was protecting—"

"Yes, that's what we thought, so we had the Magical Examiner behind the mirrored glass when we interviewed him at the station. She saw it right away."

"A geas..." Sam muttered. "Of all the rotten..." He locked eyes on Angie. "Could the defendant have been acting under a geas?"

"I'm sure Melnick will claim she was."

"How did your detectives come to be under a geas of their own?"

"That's another thing the ME discovered. They both had a few minutes of lost time— they'd forgotten the whole thing. It was one of the compulsions of the geas."

"And Angie? Me? You?"

"We'll have the ME drop by and take a look at you, Sam. She's already dispelled the geas that...blinded me." Her voice rang with fury; her expression darkened with it.

"This is terrible," murmured Sam. He gazed down at his desk for a moment, then lifted his head, eyes wide. "But who? Who did this? Who would dare? This ambassador? This Fiona..."

"Fiona Rae Gill."

Lieutenant Van Helsing floated closer. "She may be the actual target of this malcantation. We don't know for sure, and we can't force her to cooperate."

"We can arrest her!"

"She's got immunity, Sam," said Angie.

"Immunity from *prosecution*, Angie. You should know that."

"What's the point of arresting her if she's—"

"The Covenancy was not part of the Vienna Convention."

"Yes, but Canon and Covenants only take precedence when the subject is a supernatural being."

"Do we know Fiona Rae Gill is not a supernatural?"

"Sam, she holds a position in the mundane government of Ireland. Why would they—"

"Look, Angie, she's obviously taken great pains to conceal her nature."

"*If* she's a supernatural."

"Yes! But how can we know whether she's a supernatural unless we give her to the ME for Examination?"

Angie stared at him, mouth hanging open. "You can't be serious."

"Let me assure you that I am."

"Sam, the Covenant of Examination hasn't been exercised since 1692! Look how that turned out!"

"You know," said Van Helsing, "the Salem Witch Trials get a bad rap. Not all of those sweet young girls were intoxicated by the ergot fungus."

Angie whirled to face her. "Now, you can't be serious."

"My ancestors attended the Trials, and the knowledge they learned there has been passed down through our family," said Van Helsing. "I was a young girl when my father shared the tale with me, but he made sure I understood the finer points."

"Why?"

Epatha shrugged. "It was the turning point for the family, so to speak. It galvanized us to take action. After the Trials, we became...*active* hunters of evil in all its nearly infinite variations."

Angie tsked and turned her attention back to Sam. "Even if one or two of the accused were witches in breach of the Covenants, the others were innocent. Do you really want another witch hunt on your hands, Sam?"

"The Salem Witch Trials were made public—an error of great proportions." Sam nodded his head at Van Helsing. "No offence."

"None taken. My family merely *attended* the trials as official Covenancy witnesses. The whole thing would have been avoided if certain

Puritan leaders had never been allowed to read the Canon and Covenants."

Sam nodded. "No Puritans here."

"This is on your head, then," said Angie, heading for the door. "I don't want any part of it."

Sam shook his head and nodded to Van Helsing. "I trust your department will see to it? *Without* a public outcry?"

Van Helsing nodded, even as she disappeared.

IO

L eery led Dru out of the elevator and into the offices of the Irish Consulate. Danny wasn't behind the reception desk. Instead, a young woman with hair dyed the bright blue of the Caribbean sky sat filing her nails. "Help you?" she asked.

"That's not an Irish accent," said Leery. "If I had to guess, I'd say Flatbush."

"Crown Heights, but you win a prize for being close." She smiled and tilted her head to the side coquettishly.

"And what might that be?" Leery asked, smiling and sidling up to the reception desk.

"Geesh, Leery, she's young enough to be your daughter."

Leery shrugged and smiled. "It's a gift."

"It's the wolf, and you know it." Dru turned her attention to the receptionist. "We need to speak to the Ambassador."

The young woman glanced at Dru but cut her eyes back to Leery. "Anything *you* say."

Dru sighed and stared at Leery.

"Better call Ms. Gill," Leery said.

As the receptionist made the call, she pulled a pad of sticky notes over and jotted something on it. When she was finished with the call, she folded the sticky note in half and kissed it, then handed it to Leery. "Your prize."

Leery took the note and put it in his pocket, then patted the pocket.

Fiona Rae Gill came out into the lobby. "Yes, Detectives? What can I do for you today?"

"You can come with us for a start," said Leery.

Gill shook her head and hooked her thumb at the sign on the wall behind the reception desk. "I don't think so. I have diplomatic immunity."

Leery shrugged. "Hey, I just go where they say and arrest who they tell me to arrest."

"Oh, I doubt that, Detective," said the ambassador.

"Either way, you're coming with us."

The Ambassador treated them to a brittle, frosty smile. "Technically, Embassies are the sovereign property of the country which they represent. You have no jurisdiction—"

"This isn't an embassy. Did you think we wouldn't check?"

Fiona's face fell, and she opened her mouth to speak.

"Before you say anything, you should know we're now warded against manipulation," said Dru.

"I'll just get my coat. Uh…" She snapped her fingers at the blue-haired woman.

"Chastity," said the receptionist.

"Oh, now, that's a disappointment," said Leery.

"Chastity, call my deputy and ask him to arrange for an attorney. We'll be at..." She turned and quirked an eyebrow at Leery.

"The Twenty-seventh Precinct."

II

Epatha Van Helsing stood next to Leery and Dru, watching through the mirrored and warded glass of SIS's purpose-built interrogation room. Inside, Liz Hendrix stood adjusting a piece of equipment. Fiona Rae Gill sat opposite the machine, watching her closely.

"How long will this take, Lieu?" asked Leery.

"What's the matter, Oriscoe? You got another date?"

"With a girl who could be his daughter," said Dru.

"Hey, my daughter's twenty-four, so everything's legal. Besides, *she* asked *me.*"

Inside the interrogation room, Liz Hendrix straightened and turned to meet Fiona's gaze. "Do you know what this is?" she asked. Her red, red hair glistened in the overhead fluorescents.

"No, but I imagine you'll tell me."

Liz gave her a single nod, and with a glance at the mirrored window, she reached down and flipped the machine's power switch. The overhead lights flickered. "I'm going to ask you a series of questions, and I want you to answer however you'd like, as long as you speak your answer aloud."

Gill nodded, her gaze slipping away from Hendrix's and landing on the humming machine.

"What do you know of the fae?"

The ambassador scoffed. "Faery tales?"

Hendrix glanced at the machine, on which dials jumped, and lights blinked. "Hmm. Care to try again?"

"She's good," said Van Helsing. "Maybe I should fire you two and let her do all the interrogations.

"Liz can interrogate me any time she wants."

"As we are all aware to the point of nausea. Liz most of all," said Van Helsing, though she smiled at Leery as if it were all a grand joke.

"What? I bathed."

"Fiona Rae Gill, what do you know of the fae?" asked Hendrix.

The ambassador sighed and spread her hands on the table. "What any Irish woman would know."

Liz arched an eyebrow then bent and tweaked a knob on the front of her humming machine. "And what would that be?"

"You know, the Tuatha De Danann and all that. Faeries, leprechauns, aes sídhe, banshees, Dullahan, púca... Do you want me to recite all the names?"

Liz Hendrix frowned down at the machine. "Aes sídhe?"

"You know what it is."

"Okay. What do you know of witchcraft in Ireland?"

"Witchcraft? Nothing."

"Hmm." Hendrix read the dials of her machine and threw a single, startled glance at the mirrored window.

"Better get in there," said Van Helsing.

Leery was already opening the door. "Hey, Liz. I didn't know you were here. Let me buy you a cup of coffee. The lieu needs you to sign your report, by the way."

Hendrix nodded, her eyes glued to Leery's. "Sure. Coffee sounds great."

Leery glanced at the ambassador. "Just a few minutes, Ambassador Gill. Can I bring you anything? Coffee? Soda?"

"Nothing!" the woman snapped.

"Suit yourself." Leery followed Hendrix out of the room and closed the door.

"What is it?" asked Van Helsing.

"There's no doubt that thing is supernatural," said Liz. "I have no idea what, but that's no mortal woman."

12

Oriscoe led Nogan down the secret stairway from the mundane jail on Rikers Island to the Covenancy's dungeon buried beneath it. "You know most of this island is built on garbage?" he asked.

"Just like Manhattan."

"Don't worry, you won't need your rubber boots. The dungeon was dug in the original 90-acre island and lined with good ole limestone."

"Thanks for reassuring me."

Oriscoe thought he detected amusement in her tone. He shrugged and said, "Hey, that's the kind of werewolf I am. The reassuring kind."

"Yes." Again, she sounded amused, but at least this time Leery had told a joke.

At the bottom of the stone steps, they entered a small anteroom complete with fluttering torches. An elf stood behind the tall desk across from the steps. "Yes?" he asked in a bored tone.

"Oriscoe and Nogan, Supernatural Inquisition. We're here to speak to a prisoner."

"Yes?" asked the elf in the same tone.

"Delilah Lara."

"Yes."

"You know, you should see a shaman about that." Leery leaned against the desk.

"Oh? About what?"

"That stick up your ass. Might cause problems if you ever have to bend over."

The elf's face rippled with an emotion Leery couldn't name. "I'll take that under advisement, *werewolf*. Name?"

"I already told—"

"Delilah Lara," said Dru.

The elf nodded at her. "Thank you, Your Grace."

"You've got that wrong, pal. Her name's Dru."

The elf turned his ever-bored gaze on Oriscoe and curled a lip, then dismissed him with a wave. Looking at Dru, he said, "This way, *Your Grace.*"

"Thank you," said Dru. She poked Leery in the shoulder as she passed.

"Your Grace? Is there something you need to tell me, Dru?"

She threw a grimace at him over her shoulder but said nothing.

"Well, I'm not going to call you 'Your Highness,' or 'Your Grace.'"

The elf led them to one of the small rooms reserved for magisters to meet with their clients. Inside, Tovah Melnick sat beside Delilah Lara.

"Look, Dru, it's the magister for the defense."

Tovah cocked her head to the side and smiled. "You didn't think I'd allow you to meet with my client alone, did you?" Her smile seemed to imply only idiots and madmen would think so.

"Of course not. We wouldn't want to deprive Ms. Lara of her Covenantal rights."

"And where's Sam? Angie?"

"We need to ask your client a few questions, Ms. Melnick," said Dru.

"Not without a deal on the table."

"Come on, Melnick. Would we be here if McCoy hadn't ordered us here? Your client's a murderer, and we're on a tight deadline."

"Love you, too, wolfie," said Delilah in a sultry voice.

"Deli," whispered Tovah. "Still, Detective. Sam should know better."

"And I suppose this vital information couldn't be transmitted over the phone? You had to wait to tell us in person after we schlepped all the way down here from the Two Seven?"

"Ms. Melnick, we're here to help your client."

"*Help* her? Hardly." Melnick chuckled. "Tell McCoy it was a nice try."

"Relax, magister, he'll be here in a few minutes."

"Then we'll wait."

Leery drew out a chair for Dru, and when she shook her head, he sat in it.

"What's all this about?" asked Melnick.

"Let's just say things have developed in your client's case."

Melnick flashed a self-satisfied grin. "He's finally figured it out?"

At that moment, Sam and Angie came through the door. "What he's figured out, Tovah, is that your client has information we may need."

"Oh, ho!" Melnick's smile stretched. "So, Sam, what's the offer?"

"I have to hear what she has to say first."

"What would you like her to talk about?"

Angie sat down next to Leery and smiled at Melnick. "Irish folklore."

"Ah! The fae-folk, the people of the mounds."

"Just so," said Sam.

"And what's this history lesson worth to you?"

"History? Nothing. Depending on what your client has to say, however, it may be worth a reduced sentence."

Tovah folded arms across her chest. "She walks, Sam."

"For murder? Never gonna happen, Tovah."

"If you're here, you know about the geas," said Tovah with a shrewd look in her eye. "A reduced charge and probation."

Sam shrugged. "Telling us things we already know gets your client nothing, Tovah."

Melnick smiled and nodded to Delilah. "Go ahead, Deli."

"But he hasn't said what the deal will be."

"And he won't—not until he hears what you have to say. But you can trust Sam. Or if you can't, you can trust me."

Deli nodded, then yawned. "She's a fetch."

"Who is?"

"You know who!" snapped Delilah. "It's written all over you."

Sam squinted down at her but gave her a slow nod. "Ambassador Fiona Rae Gill."

"The very one."

"And that means the real Fiona Rae Gill is dead?" asked Angie.

"It could be," said Delilah with a shrug. "Or she could be on ice somewhere here or back in Ireland."

Sam shook his head and shrugged. "But why?"

"Why do any of us do anything?" asked Deli. "It is her nature."

Sam ran a hand through his salt-and-pepper hair. "Better tell us all of it."

"It was a geas, as you already know," said Delilah. "She didn't think she needed to waste energy making me forget or stopping me from speaking out. She figured you would see a man killed by a succubus, find a succubus, and convict her without looking too deeply." She nodded at Leery and Dru. "She put a geas on these two to make sure they didn't ask the wrong questions."

"And those wrong questions are?"

Deli shrugged and smiled. "Why an aunt would want her nephew to be killed, for one."

"And what's the answer?"

"Because the boy was suspicious of her. A fetch can only carry off the illusion if no one looks very deeply."

"I don't get it," said Leery. "Why—"

"I bet you get it all the time, wolfie," said Deli with a wink.

"—would she care? Why take over the life of an Ambassador to the UN?"

"*An Roinn Gnóthaí Eachtracha agus Trádála*," murmured Dru. "The Department of Foreign Affairs and Trade."

Deli nodded, and a smug smile spread across her face.

"So, these fetches want better tariffs?" asked Leery with a shake of his head.

"No, Oriscoe," said Sam. "But they want free and unfettered trade with other countries."

"Why?"

"That's the question, isn't it?" asked Deli.

"What's your guess?"

Deli shrugged and smiled a secretive smile. "I think they want it to be easier to hitch a ride to another country."

"Hitch a ride?"

"Take someone's identity."

13

Sam and Angie stepped off the elevator. Sam headed for his office, eyeing the short man in the black sweat suit nosing around his office door with suspicion. "Can I help you?"

"I'm looking for Sam McCoy."

"You've found him."

The man smiled and pulled a blue packet of papers from the pocket of his pants. "You've been served, McCoy."

Sam shrugged, took the papers, and handed them to Angie. "Next time, skip the cloak and dagger. I'm an officer of the Magical Court. You can leave the summons with my secretary."

The man smirked and headed for the elevator.

"How much trouble are we in?" Sam asked Angie.

She handed the summons to Sam. "Gill is asserting her diplomatic immunity."

"That's ridiculous. First, she's not really Fiona Rae Gill. Second, she's a supernatural, and the Canon and Covenants—"

"You don't have to convince *me*, Sam. You have to convince the Locus Court of Appeals tomorrow at nine."

"Then we'd better get busy."

14

The next morning at 9:20 a.m., Sam stood in the appellate chamber. As per usual for such occasions, he carried nothing, had brought nothing, needed nothing.

He approached the lectern with its three lights: green for when you have all the time in the world, yellow for when time grows short, and red for when you're out of time. A part of him preferred the rules of a case like this in the appellate court, the enforced brevity, no witnesses to muddy the waters, no jury.

"Mr. McCoy? Are you ready to begin?"

"Sorry, Your Honor. Just woolgathering."

"Indeed? At a time like this?"

"My apologies, Your Honor. As the years pass, woolgathering becomes less an indulgence and more a surprise."

"Yes. Time finds us all in the end. This time, however, is yours, Mr. McCoy."

"Yes, Your Honor." McCoy stepped up to the lectern, resting one hand on either side of it, and cleared his throat. "If it pleases the Court, my name is Executive Locus Magister Sam

McCoy, and I stand before you this morning on a matter of dire importance. My opponent alleges his client is a diplomat, and as such, should be accorded diplomatic immunity. If you will, please allow me to explain the ludicrousness of the argument.

"First and foremost, we must examine the nature of the plaintiff. This creature, pretending even now to be Fiona Rae Gill of Ireland, is *not* Fiona Rae Gill, but rather a fetch of unknown identity. She's taken the real Ms. Gill's place in the world. Indeed, we've contacted the Irish authorities, and no one can say where the real Ms. Gill is at present. We suspect she's left this plane for those beyond."

"But you have no proof of this?"

"Your Honor, it's true we have no proof whether Ms. Gill still breathes, but we have mountains of evidence supporting the nature of the creature sitting at the table to my left."

"And the nature of this evidence?"

"If it pleases the Court, I don't wish to disclose the entirety of the evidence we've amassed, as pending criminal proceedings—"

"I object, Your Honors. There has been no complaint filed against my client. She's merely been arrested and detained—"

"Begging the Court's pardon, my colleague is in error. My office filed formal charges against a Jane Doe defendant this morning in circuit court. The plaintiff is the Jane Doe in question. Papers have been dispatched, but evidently not served as of yet. I have officers waiting outside to return this creature into the custody of the dungeon located on Rikers Island, where her powers may be mitigated by old wards, often reinforced." A flurry of whispering erupted from the prosecution table, and Sam fought to contain his mirth.

"Very well, Mr. McCoy."

"Thank you, Your Honor. Given that this is not Fiona Rae Gill, and that the Irish government has endowed Fiona Rae Gill, and *only* Ms. Gill, as their Ambassador to the United Nations, this creature has no claim to diplomatic immunity. Her diplomatic passport, as is the ambassadorship, is Ms. Gill's alone, and it does *not* extend to a creature assuming her identity. I've confirmed this with the Irish government, as evidenced by the letter included in my motion."

"Your Honor, I must object," said the magister for the fetch. "Whatever their intentions were, the officials of the Irish government swore my client in as the ambassador, issued her the passport bearing her own image—and this can be verified by the Locus Magical Examiner, surely. Regardless of their intent, my client, the fetch currently known as Fiona Rae Gill, *is the Irish Ambassador to the United Nations.*"

"Mr. McCoy?"

"Thank you, Your Honor. My learned colleague has forgotten basic Canon and Covenant. The acts he described represented an unprecedented fraud perpetrated by his client by magical means, and no supernatural being can legally benefit from improper actions."

"I dispute the actions are improper, Your Honors. The Covenants define improper action as those acts that deprive another of their rights *unless* said action is required for the maintenance of life, as dictated by the nature of the supernatural being. My client is a fetch. She lives solely to assume the lives of other beings, endeavoring to make the world a better place by acting with a pearl of wisdom mere mortals cannot hope to match."

"I'm willing to bet Eddie Thompson doesn't consider her actions all that wise."

"Then prove she murdered the man!" snapped the other magister.

"I will," said Sam. "But to do so, your client must be charged."

"My client is not a succubus. Eddie Thompson was drained by a succubus. In fact, the Locus Magister has already charged one Delilah Lara with the murder, and the case is before Judge Crowley in circuit court."

The lead judge looked at Sam and crooked his shaggy white eyebrow. "Mr. McCoy?"

"Charges are indeed pending against Ms. Lara, but the court stands in recess until this matter is resolved and the possibility of a plea bargain is explored with Ms. Lara and counsel."

"You allege the plaintiff has manipulated Ms. Lara…via magical means or otherwise."

"Yes, Your Honor. The creature to my left cast a geas on her. And not only on her, but also on two members of the Supernatural Inquisitors Squad, an Assistant Locus Magister, and myself."

"You've evidence to support this geas?"

"I do, Your Honor, in the form of expert testimony from the Magical Examiner."

"Very well, Mr. McCoy. Proceed with your argument."

"Yes, Your Honor. The second point we must consider is that even if we grant this fetch's claim at legitimacy based on her fraud, as a supernatural, diplomatic immunity does not extend to her. The Covenancy did not ratify the Vienna Convention, and, thus, supernatural beings are not protected by it."

"An interesting argument. Anything else?"

"No, Your Honor. I thank the Court for its time this morning and look forward to the forthcoming ruling."

"Very well. This court stands in recess." The craggy-browed head judge banged his gavel.

15

Sam sat in his office, trying to work but unable to focus on anything but the ticking clock on his credenza. He swiveled in his chair and stared out the window, watching the first eddies of snow drift earthward. A knock captured his attention, and he turned back to see the Locus Magister, Adam Hill, standing in his doorway. "Hello, Adam."

"Sam. I wanted to be the first to congratulate you."

"On?" Sam's pulse and respiration quickened, though he tried to appear aloof.

"The appellate court published its opinion. The vote was unanimous."

"Don't tease me, Adam!"

"You'd better start preparing to prosecute the fetch. Her petition for diplomatic immunity was denied, and she remains in custody pending trial."

Sam breathed a sigh of relief and sank back in his chair.

"Merlin himself complemented your arguments in the ruling. Nice work."

"Thanks, Adam."

"Don't screw up the murder trial."

"And thanks for the vote of confidence."

Adam smiled, donned his black woolen hat, fluffed his *payot*, turned, and left with a smile on his face.

Sam smiled his secret smile and got to work.

16

Opening statements in the case against the fetch known as Jane Doe went as Sam had expected. He outlined the case against her, and her assigned defense magister, Geoffery Laveau, squandered his time with hyper-technical (and incorrect) interpretations of both the mundane diplomacy law and the Canon and Covenants. Sam had watched the jury as this opening statement unfolded and was pleased to see them fighting to stay awake.

Laveau was new to the supernatural defender's office, and this would be his first case in which the charges spanned beyond class E felonies. Sam almost felt sorry for the fetch—as her identity as Fiona Rae Gill was proved false, she had no access to funds and no way to call on the Irish government for legal support.

Then again, she'd cast a geas on him, and that still rankled.

The fetch sat slumped behind the defense table, still in the guise of Fiona Rae Gill, but

Sam was told to expect that—she'd be trapped in that form until she waylaid another poor sap.

"Mr. McCoy? Are you ready to proceed with your case?"

"Yes, Your Honor." They'd drawn Judge Crowley again, and that pleased Sam. He was a burning judge, and everyone knew it. Of course, he hadn't sentenced anyone to the stake since the Locus had forbidden executions, but he seemed to delight in handing down judgments so severe they seemed to teeter on the edge of callousness and spitefulness.

Sam turned to the bailiff. "The People call Liz Hendrix, Locus Magical Examiner."

There was a soft hustle and bustle as Hendrix took the stand and was sworn in. Sam spent the time smiling benevolently at the jury—it was an expression he practiced in the mirror, and he was proud of it.

"Ms. Hendrix, you serve the Locus of New York in the capacity of Magical Examiner, do you not?"

"I do."

"Very well. Could you refresh the jury's memory of what your position entails?"

"Certainly. In the normal course of supernatural criminal investigations, many things arise that require a critical eye. A more theoretical knowledge of magic than many of our Warders on the police force have. Which is not to say I'm a better witch. I'm not, not at all. I couldn't do what Warders do, just as they are not suited to do what I do."

"And what kinds of things do you do on a day to day basis?"

"I might be called on to read the aura of the recently deceased."

"And do you speak to their spirits?"

"No, sir. I'm not a medium." She inclined her head toward Judge Crowley in salute to his past accomplishments in the field. "If I were, I'd be a member of the Conjuration, Scrying, and Invocation."

"Then what information can you learn from this aural reading?"

"Time of death, manner of death, sometimes the victim's state of mind at the time of death."

Sam nodded and turned to the jury, his benevolent smile in place and turned up a notch. "And in the case before the Court?"

"Yes, I determined all three things I mentioned."

"Tell us, please, the state of mind of the victim."

"Your Honor, I object," said Laveau, standing and shuffling through a messy stack of papers.

They waited, and when he failed to state his reason for objecting, Judge Crowley leaned forward, inclined his head, and peered at the supernatural defender from under brows wrinkled with pique. "Mr. Laveau, it is customary to have your arguments in order *before* raising your objections."

"Yes, Judge. If you'll give me one moment…"

Crowley's frown deepened until his stare became a glower. "By all means, Mr. Laveau. *Take your time.*"

Laveau missed his tone or simply didn't care. Sam watched him search through his notes with a bemused smile twitching his lips.

"*Mr. Laveau*," said Crowley. "I'm clairvoyant to a high degree and well-versed in my art, but even I have no idea what you object to."

"Yes, Your Honor. Sorry, Your Honor. I…uh…I object on the grounds that my client didn't directly murder the victim. Even McCoy admits this."

Sam waited, watching Crowley's form flicker as his anger grew.

"Mr. Laveau, if you'd allow him to go on, Mr. McCoy was no doubt about to establish that as a fact of the record." He turned to McCoy and lifted his eyebrow.

"Indeed, Your Honor."

"Oh...uh... In that case, I withdraw my objection."

"*Your Honor*," hissed Crowley.

"I beg your pardon?" asked Laveau, glancing around as though for help. Or a place to hide.

"*I withdraw my objection, Your Honor!*"

"Yes, Your Honor. Apologies. I withdraw my objection, Your Honor."

"Fine!" snapped Crowley. "Go ahead, Mr. McCoy."

"Thank you, Your Honor." Sam stood for a moment, head cocked to the side, gazing at Laveau and wondering what his game was. Or if he was really as stupid as he appeared.

"Mr. McCoy?"

Sam turned back to Liz Hendrix. "Ms. Hendrix, were you able, in the case before the court, to establish the time and method of death, as well as the victim's state of mind?"

"Yes, I was."

"Would you share his final mortal thoughts?"

"Yes, Mr. McCoy. Edward Thompson, nineteen, died in the ecstasy of coitus, but even during that act, a part of his mind bore significant anxiety regarding the fetch acting as his aunt."

"And to what did you originally attribute this anxiety?"

Hendrix's cheeks colored. "Well, he died in the arms of a succubus and one he paid. I believed his anxiety was attributable to the shame of being caught."

"Do you still believe that?"

Hendrix shook her head. "No. After certain discoveries regarding the state of mind of Detectives Oriscoe and Nogan, I—"

"You refer to the geas placed on the detectives by the defendant?"

"At that time, I didn't know who placed it, but there was indeed a geas."

"A magical compulsion?"

"Yes."

Sam spread his hands. "To what end?"

"To facilitate a rush to judgment against the succubus who committed the act."

"And were others affected by a similar geas?"

Hendrix nodded. "Yes. Two members of the Locus Magisters office, the detective's lieutenant, and the succubus who committed the act, Delilah Lara."

"I see. And were the purposes of all these compulsions the same?"

"No, the spells affecting your assistant and you were to bend you to resist a plea bargain and to think your case was stronger than it was."

The jury stirred, and pencils flittered across notepads.

Sam glanced at Angie. "To think it was a 'slam dunk' in colloquial parlance?"

"Yes."

"And the compulsion placed on Ms. Lara?"

"Hers was both more and less complex."

"How so?" asked McCoy.

"She was driven to accept the boy's advances, to acquiesce to his desires, and once the act began, to continue past the point of safety."

"To kill him, in other words."

"Yes, by draining his lifeforce past critical levels."

"And how was her geas less complex than those placed on myself and my colleagues?"

"She was not ordered to forget its casting."

"And the members of law enforcement were?"

"Yes. In normal cases, the victim of a geas is fully cognizant of the spell and the caster. Not so in this case, as such knowledge would obviously conflict with the goals of the geas in the case of the detectives."

"Very well. Am I still under the effects of the defendant's geas?"

Laveau shot to his feet. "I object, Your Honor! Mr. McCoy hasn't established his geas—nor any other—was cast by my client."

"Mr. McCoy?" asked Crowley.

"I'll rectify that at once."

"Carry on. Objection overruled pending Mr. McCoy's next few questions."

"Ms. Hendrix, were you able to trace any of these compulsions?"

"Not magically, but I was able to trace them to the defendant."

"Then how did you do so?"

"Markers in the magical field surrounding all five victims prior to lifting the spells matched. I interviewed the victims, and

Delilah Lara, as I mentioned a moment ago, remembered being geased by the defendant."

"So, because the markers matched and Ms. Lara claims to remember who cast the spell, you concluded that all five victims were manipulated by the fetch?"

"Yes."

McCoy turned to Crowley. "Is that sufficient, Your Honor?"

"I'm convinced," said Crowley.

Sam wanted to wince but restrained himself. With a competent magister, that statement might create grounds for appeal. He glanced at Laveau, who sat watching with a placid expression on his face as though he were dreaming of more pleasant surroundings. "Ms. Hendrix, did you also have occasion to meet with the defendant?"

"I did. The Supernatural Inquisitors Squad at the Twenty-seventh Precinct asked me to Examine the defendant. I understand this was at your request."

"It was."

"*Witch trials*?" blurted Laveau.

McCoy shook his head.

"Is that an objection, Mr. Laveau?"

"Sorry, Your Honor. It's just so...so..."

"Unusual?" Judge Crowley turned to McCoy. "You walk a dangerous edge, Mr. McCoy."

"Yes, Your Honor, but precautions were taken."

"Very well."

"Thank you, Judge Crowley." Sam turned back to Liz Hendrix. "Can you explain to the Court how you undertook to Examine the defendant?"

"With pleasure. I employed a bit of subterfuge in the form of extra equipment from the ME's office. That is, I used an aural recording device during the interview, but I had enchanted my sense to perceive the defendant at a high level of detail."

"And this led you to conclude the defendant was a fetch?"

"No, but there was incontrovertible evidence that she was a supernatural."

"I see." McCoy turned and looked at Laveau, and again, the man seemed to be daydreaming. "Your witness, Mr. Laveau."

"What?" His gaze drifted around the courtroom for a heartbeat, then settled on Hendrix, and his eyes cleared. "Yes. Just a few questions, Your Honor."

"Then, by all means, go on."

Laveau stood and approached the witness box. "Ms. Hendrix, are you, in your capacity as Magical Examiner, able to offer statistics regarding the error rate of Magical Examiners when assessing these markers in the magical field you mentioned?"

"Yes, there have been errors in the past."

"By your office?"

"No."

"By you at another office."

"Not to my knowledge."

"But mistakes *do* happen."

"The incidence rate is one in six hundred forty-three thousand, Mr. Laveau." She peered up at him.

"But not zero, is it?"

"No. Like I said, it's one in six hundred forty-three thousand."

"More of an art than a science?"

Hendrix stared at him through narrowed eyelids. "Not at all. Those are significant statistics, and they led to the acceptance of Magical Field studies as a science in every Locus on the planet." She cocked her head to the side. "Are you aware of it?"

He frowned at her and pulled his head back like a bird trying to get a better look at her. "I'll ask the questions."

"The geas, I mean. Are you aware that you've been geased?"

The courtroom fell silent, with not even a gasp coming from the gallery. McCoy got to his feet. "Your Honor?"

"My chambers!" snapped Crowley. "Ms. Hendrix, if you please."

"I object, Your Honor. She's still my sworn witness," said Laveau.

"Overruled."

17

Judge Crowley's chambers were plush but furnished in styles from the Roaring Twenties and the Locus of London. The judge stomped behind his desk, waving his hand and unburdening himself from his spectral black robes. "This had better not be a prank!" he snapped at McCoy, then turned and glared at Angie Carmichael.

"I know nothing about this, Your Honor."

Crowley's gaze skimmed past Laveau and settled on Liz Hendrix. "You say he's under a geas? Can you determine what the purpose of it is?"

"It's complex, Your Honor." She peered at Laveau and muttered a spell under her breath. "The field matches, though. The fetch did this."

"It's fine," said Laveau. "I know all about it."

"You do?" asked Crowley. "Then you'd better explain it to me. Right now."

"It's personal."

Crowley faded in and out at a rapid pace, and his eyes grew wide. "Contempt of court, Mr. Laveau, will not look good on your resume."

"Yes, Your Honor," he said.

Crowley waited, pulsing in and out of phase. "And?" he demanded.

"I...was...curious."

"*Your Honor!*" snapped Crowley.

"Yes, Your Honor. Apologies."

"Curious about what?" asked Sam.

"Whether she could really geas *anyone*. I wanted... I've never met a psychopomp, even one not all twisted around like a fetch is. I wanted to see her power for myself." He shook his head. "I wanted to see if I could withstand the geas."

"Mr. Laveau!"

"But don't worry," he said in a rush. "It's benign. The geas."

Crowley arched an eyebrow at Hendrix.

"No, Your Honor, it isn't. Part of it seems bent toward making him believe it to be so, but the other part, the *deeper* part...is...confusing. I can't tell if he's to throw the case and then allow her to take his place, or..." She leaned toward Laveau, squinting. "Definitely not benign, Mr. Laveau."

"You're a foolish young man, aren't you?" mused Crowley. "To put yourself into the power of one such as she. Did your parents fail to teach you common sense?"

"My parents died when I was young. I was raised by my grandmother in New Orleans. She's—"

"I'm sure this is interesting," said Crowley. "But not germane. Well, Ms. Hendrix? Can you remove this geas?"

She tore her eyes away from Laveau and treated Crowley to a single bob of her head. "I can."

"Then do so."

"Wait just a minute!" hissed Laveau. "I don't give my permission. She's not to use magic on me!"

"She will, and you will not fight her," said Crowley in a voice that rang like hot steel under the hammer. "Under the influence of your client, the fetch, your judgment is unreliable. Mine will suffice until the geas is removed, and you have recovered."

"Um..." Liz Hendrix darted a glance at McCoy, then arched her eyebrow.

"Problems, Ms. Magical Examiner?" asked Crowley in the same tone of voice.

Sam gave an almost imperceptible nod.

"None, Your Honor," said Liz as she set about removing the geas. When she finished, she turned and nodded to Judge Crowley.

"Very good. How do you feel, Mr. Laveau?"

"Furious with my client, Your Honor. I wish to be removed."

"Denied. If you were foolish enough to allow her to put a compulsion on you, you can live with your emotions. Though I expect you to fulfill your duties under the Canon and Covenants. Is that clear, Mr. Laveau?"

"It is, Your Honor."

"Very well then, ladies and gentlemen, we're going to return to my courtroom and proceed with this trial." He glowered at Geoffery Laveau. "I do not expect any additional tom-foolery from the magisters. No more senseless objections, no daydreaming, no putting yourselves in the power of this fetch, who has now managed to geas half the Locus it seems."

Laveau's expression remained stricken as they all filed back toward the courtroom. Before he entered, he tapped Liz on the shoulder. "Thank you," he said in muted tones.

"Anytime, Counselor."

18

Judge Crowley called the court to order, then turned to the jury. "It's my duty to give you the following instruction. In assessing the guilt or innocence of the defendant, you are to disregard the last exchange between the defense magister and this witness, to wit, you will disregard the geas placed on the defense magister by his client. It has been rectified and is not evidence in this proceeding and will not be admitted as such." He turned to Liz Hendrix, then to Laveau and McCoy, each in his turn. "We will not mention it again in front of the jury." When no one objected, he gave the entire room a single nod, then motioned at Laveau. "Your witness, I believe, Mr. Laveau."

"Uh, yes. Thank you, Your Honor." Laveau got to his feet and approached the witness stand once more. "We were speaking of the error rate in the identification and study of magical fields."

Liz nodded. "We were."

"You had just explained that the low incidence of error led to the wide acceptance of the field in scientific and legal circles."

"That's correct."

"Very well. Let's leave the general cases aside for the moment. Can you be one hundred percent certain in your analysis?"

"There's always the small chance of an error, but in this case, I was meticulous in my method. I can say with a high level of confidence that my analysis is spot on."

Laveau dropped his chin and fiddled with the pen he held. "Very well. Can you explain why you, a trained Magical Examiner, could not understand the nature of my client?"

"Your Honor, I—"

"I'll allow it, Mr. McCoy."

"Yes, Your Honor."

Liz cocked her head and looked past Laveau to gaze at the fetch. "Simply put, there are two reasons. First, the Covenant of Examination hasn't been enacted since the Salem Witch Trials to my knowledge. That type of Magical Examination is treated as a theoretical topic in schools, and no practical education in the matter is proffered. Second, the defendant's type is exceedingly rare—and growing more so as the old faiths fall away, and psychopomps are disbelieved by more and more people."

"Ah, I see. So, you weren't educated in the identification of supernatural beings, and even if you were, you wouldn't have known much about the fetch in general."

"That's correct."

"Yet, you stand by your identification?"

"I didn't name her as a fetch, only as a supernatural, and the disruptions she caused in the ether under questioning were plain to see."

"Yet, the detectives didn't pick up on it."

"I can't speak to that."

"Because they should have, and you wish to protect them?"

"Your Honor!" said McCoy, leaping to his feet.

"It's okay," said Liz. "I'd like to answer that."

"You may, Ms. Hendrix," said Crowley as he motioned Sam back into his seat.

"Not at all, Mr. Laveau. I can't speak to it because I have no direct knowledge that Detectives Oriscoe and Nogan didn't consider the defendant a supernatural."

"No direct..." muttered Laveau.

"What was that, Mr. Laveau?"

"Oh, nothing, Your Honor. I have no more questions for this witness, though I reserve the right to recall Ms. Hendrix at a later date, should impeaching evidence arise."

"It is your right," said Crowley. "You may step down, Ms. Hendrix, with the thanks of this Court." After Hendrix left, he turned to McCoy and arched his eyebrows.

McCoy nodded and stood. "The prosecution calls Detective Leery Oriscoe, Your Honor."

Leery took the stand with a grin.

"Detective Oriscoe, do you recognize the defendant?"

"I do."

"From where?"

"The defendant is a fetch, taking the place of Fiona Rae Gill, the rightful Ambassador to the United Nations for the country of Ireland."

"I object, Your Honor," said Laveau. "This witness is no expert in Foreign Affairs, nor is he a Covenant scholar."

McCoy raised one hand, index finger pointing at the sky and a victorious smile decorating his face. "He doesn't need to be, Your Honor. The identity of the fetch and the fraud she perpetrated on the Irish government is a matter of record. The opinion of the Locus Court of Appeals can be entered as evidence and read into the record if the Court desires it."

Sam glanced at Laveau, who seemed to have turned a little green.

"Overruled, Mr. Laveau. I'd recommend you keep up on the rulings of the appellate court as they relate to your own cases."

"Yes. Thank you, Your Honor."

With a satisfied expression, McCoy turned back to the jury. "You were saying, Detective?"

"The defendant is a fetch. She's assumed the life of Fiona Rae Gill."

"And is Ms. Gill still with us, Detective?"

"That's unknown at this time. If she is, she can't be located using the full resources of both the NYPD and the Irish government."

"Thank you, Detective Oriscoe. Can you describe the circumstances of your first meeting with the defendant?"

"We were pursuing the case of the murder of Edward Thompson, a native of Ireland. The kid was here on a visitor's visa. He appears to have been mundane. We visited the defendant's offices, hoping to find information about Thompson's next of kin."

"And did you find such?"

"We did. The defendant stated Mr. Thompson was the nephew of Ms. Gill."

"And did you learn anything else?"

"Yes. We spoke with the defendant's receptionist, who stated he'd taken the victim on a tour through a few of the seedier clubs in Times Square."

"Sex clubs?"

"Sure, you could call them that."

"Very well. Subsequent to that information, were you able to trace the victim's movements?"

"Yes. We found he'd had business with a succubus named Delilah Lara. She later confessed to having drained the victim of his lifeforce."

"Did she say anything else?"

"Not at that time."

"Very well. How long did you spend with the defendant?"

"That first time? It seemed like ten minutes, but in reality, it was closer to twenty."

"What happened in the balance of the time?"

"She put a compulsion on my partner and me."

"A geas."

"Yes."

"That's all I have, Your Honor."

"Very well, Mr. McCoy. Mr. Laveau?"

"Thank you, Judge." Crowley stood next to the defense table. "Detective Oriscoe, you say the meeting felt like ten minutes?"

"Yes."

"But was more like twenty?"

"Yes."

"Did you report that in your notes? In your original arrest report of Ms. Lara?"

"No and no."

"And why was that?"

Leery smiled. "I didn't remember it. Not then."

"But you remember it now?" Laveau leaned forward on the balls of his feet.

"Yeah. That's how the geas worked. It commanded us not to remember the defendant casting the spell."

"You couldn't remember then, but you can remember now?"

"That's right, Counselor."

"Correct me if I'm wrong, Detective, but you're no warlock. You're a shapeshifter?"

"Sure. My werewolf half is a Black Hat, but I don't guess you're going to ask me about Kabbalah."

"No. How do you know?"

"How do I know you're not going to ask me about Kabbalah? Just a guess, really."

"Your Honor, I move to strike as nonresponsive."

"So ordered." Crowley turned and glowered at Oriscoe. "Detective, you've been doing this a long time. You know better."

Oriscoe grimaced and sighed. "Yes, Your Honor. I'll be good."

Crowley continued to stare at him a moment, then shifted his gaze to Laveau. "Continue."

"Detective, if you are no warlock, how do you know the geas affected your memory?"

"I'll say it slow and use little words for you, Counselor. I know because—"

"*Detective*," murmured Crowley, but the power behind the whisper carried his words to every ear, every corner of the courtroom.

"Sorry, Judge. I know because I *remember* the geas, Counselor."

"Ah, I see. We're back to that curiously infallible memory of yours."

Oriscoe flashed a bitter, sarcastic smile at him. "Now, you're on my scent."

Laveau sighed. "Very well, Detective. Can you think of a reason why a succubus facing conviction for murder would lie to incriminate my client?"

"One reason? No. Thirty or forty? Sure, but that doesn't mean Delilah Lara is lying."

"Is there proof to back her spurious claims?"

"We're here, aren't we?"

Laveau sighed and looked to the jury as if to ask if they could see what he had to deal with.

"Very well, Detective. Your Honor, I have no further questions for this...witness."

"You may step down, Detective Oriscoe. The Court thanks you for your testimony—the parts of it that remain in the record."

"Thanks, Your Honor."

As Leery passed the prosecution table, Sam spoke without looking up. "You've still got it, Leery."

"Don't I just?" Leery murmured back.

Sam stood and faced the bench. "If it pleases the court, the People call Detective Drusilla Nogan."

Crowley gave him an unreadable look but waved his hand at the bailiff. As Nogan entered and was sworn in, the judge stared up at the ceiling in pensive silence.

Nogan took her seat in the witness box, and Sam stood and took a few steps forward. Before he could speak, however, Crowley held up a translucent hand and gestured for him to stop.

"Before I allow your examination of this witness, the Court wishes to welcome Her Grace and thank her for her willingness to testify in the sordid affair."

Dru nodded.

"This is off the record," he said to the clerk. "Your Grace, I wish to extend proper courtesy, but my position and yours makes that impossible at present." He tilted his head to the side. "How is Her Grace, your royal mother?"

"She's fine, Aleister, as always."

"Give her my best."

"I'll be sure to do so the next time I speak to her."

"Your Grace, if you feel uncomfortable with any question, do not hesitate to let me know, and I will strike it from the record."

"Thank you, Aleister, but I'm sure everyone will behave."

"Oh, they will, Your Grace. I promise you that." He took a moment to glower at both the defense and the prosecution, then waved McCoy forward. "Back on the record, clerk."

Sam turned and glanced at Angie with raised eyebrows, but she only shrugged. With a shrug of his own, he turned back to Nogan. "Detective Nogan, with your permission, I'll begin my direct examination."

"Please."

Sam's questions for Dru bore a striking resemblance to his questions for Leery, and her answers also resembled those given by Leery to a high degree. The direct examination ended without a single objection raised by Laveau.

"Mr. Laveau, do you have questions for Her Royal Highness?"

"Yes, Your Honor."

"I warn you to show proper respect."

"Er, yes, Your Honor." Laveau stood and approached the witness box. "Detective Nogan, that's not your *true* name, is it?"

Dru arched an eyebrow and glanced at Aleister Crowley.

"Strike that from the record!" he barked, then leveled a finger at Laveau. "I'm warning you, warlock."

"Yes, Your Honor." Laveau again glanced at the jury, this time with a long-suffering sigh. "Detective, uh, Nogan, you are..." He glanced at Crowley, who narrowed his eyes. "No, strike that, please. Detective Nogan, are you familiar with witchcraft at a more than amateur level?"

Dru stared at him for one moment, then treated him to a slow, somehow regal, nod. "I'm a Warder for the Supernatural Inquisitors Squad of the NYPD. As such, I'm well-versed in the topic."

"Of course, of course. Tell me, why didn't you ward your partner and yourself better, and having failed to do so, why didn't you recognize the spell casting and stop it?"

Crowley growled from the bench and began to flicker.

"It's all right, Aleis—Your Honor," Dru murmured. Her gaze rested on Laveau as she answered. "I made a mistake with the warding. We didn't expect to find anything other than bureaucracy, and we certainly didn't expect to find a supernatural."

"A mistake?"

"Yes, it was my first case with SIS, and I made a mistake. One I won't repeat."

"I'm sure." Laveau smirked at the jury. "And tell me, Detective, did you also suffer from the curious malady of memory that Detective Oriscoe testified to?"

"I have no idea how my partner testified. We didn't discuss it beforehand."

"As is only proper," said Crowley, smiling down at her like a proud uncle.

"The Locus Magister's office didn't prepare the two of you? Didn't tell you what to say and how to say it?"

"No. Are you accusing me of perjury?"

Laveau held up his hands and reared back like a carnival huckster about to deliver a punchline. "No, of course, not. The LM's office and the police force are beyond such things."

"That's it," said Crowley in a flat tone. "Your examination of this witness is over, Laveau."

With another conspiratorial glance at the jury, Laveau inclined his head. "Of course, it is, Your Honor." Again, he sighed in a dramatic manner, then turned on his heel and returned to the defense table.

Crowley glared at him throughout his performance and only shifted his gaze after Laveau sat down and smiled at him. The judge turned to face Dru. "I apologize on behalf of the Court, Your Grace. Laveau is new to my courtroom and evidently doesn't understand the rules of proper comportment."

"Thank you, Your Honor," she said, treating him to a bright smile.

"You may step down with thanks from both the Court and this old spirit." He waved at the clerk. "Off the record." Turning back to Dru, he treated her to his "uncle smile" once more. "It was delightful to see you, Your Highness. I hope to see you again, but without such a long hiatus."

"I'm sure we will see each other again soon, Aleister."

"Quite. Stop by anytime." He watched her leave the box and walk through the gallery, his gaze a fond one. When the door swung shut behind her, he turned to the clerk. "On the record, again. Mr. McCoy, I see that your next witness is Delilah Lara. As I expect her direct and cross-examinations will be time-consuming, court is adjourned until nine tomorrow morning."

19

Sam and Angie walked down the steps of the courthouse. "Her Royal Highness?" Sam asked.

"I've got no idea. In Texas, the only royals we have are a women's spirit group at UT Austin."

"Crowley didn't want her identity on record."

"No," said Angie, looking down and letting her sable hair cascade in front of her face.

"Though he certainly made a big deal of her rank."

"Strange, isn't it?"

"You bet. I never have understood mediums. *Or* ghosts."

"It seems like a thing we should know. Have Her Royal Highness come by the office in thirty minutes."

Angie nodded and peeled away to make the call. Sam gazed down at the sidewalk in front of him and shook his head.

20

Leery looked across his desk at Dru as she spoke on the phone. He'd already been filled in about Crowley's behavior in court, and his curiosity was eating him alive. Every time Dru glanced at him, he pretended he was looking at something over her shoulder, but he didn't think she was buying it.

"What?" she demanded when she hung up the phone.

"Who? Me?"

Dru rolled her eyes. "That was the LM's office with some bullshit. I've got something to take care of. I'll see you tomorrow, Leery."

"Alone? They don't need me?"

"No, just me." She stood and turned her back, pulling on her coat.

"Whatever you say, Princess," Leery muttered.

She heaved a sigh and turned back. "I don't suppose you can pretend..." She shook her head. "I guess you deserve to know." She tsked and rolled her eyes. "So much for my secret identity." She sat down and leaned across her desk, motioning him closer. "My real name is Drusilla bat Agrat."

Leery shrugged. "I like Nogan better."

"You don't recognize the name?"

"Bat Agrat? No, never heard it."

"In this case, 'bat' means 'daughter of.'"

"Drusilla, daughter of... Oh."

"Right. My mother is Agrat bat Mahlat, one of the Four Queens of Hell."

"Oh," Leery repeated.

She watched him through squinted eyes. "Is this going to be a thing?"

"Er… No, not at all," said Leery as if he met demonic royalty every day.

She sighed and shook her head. "Yes, it is."

"No, really, Dru. I don't care." He arched his neck and rubbed his temples. "But it makes sense of certain things."

"Yes," sighed Dru.

"You know, in Hebrew, your grandmother's name can also mean illusion."

"Yes."

"And your mother is called the Witch Queen."

"Yes."

"But your father is a vampire."

"Yes."

"Not Samael."

"No, his name is Hercule."

"A Frenchman? Go figure. You hardly look like the paintings of Asmodeus, anyway."

She treated him to a tentative smile.

"Really, Dru. It's fine. If you want me to pretend not to know…"

"No, that's silly. Just don't start with the 'Your Grace' or 'Your Highness' crap. I'll take it from Aleister, but he's like a kindly old uncle to me."

"You got it, kid."

With a wink and smile, she got up and left. At the door, she turned and frowned. "And don't tell Van Helsing," she mouthed in silence.

Leery nodded and pretended to zip his lips shut.

21

Adam Hill knocked and came into Sam's office through the side door. He wasn't holding his hat and coat, and he had his shirt sleeves rolled up.

"Adam," said Sam. "I'm about to go into a meeting—"

Adam waved his hand in an arc. "No, you're not."

Sam frowned. "I have Detective—"

"She's not coming, I said."

"What's going on here, Adam?"

"Some things are above your pay grade, Sam. Some things I get to tell you and don't have to tell you why."

Sam huffed and shook his head. "If she's—"

"Sam," said Adam, stepping into the office and closing the door behind him. "You don't need to know. You probably don't *want* to know, either. I certainly wish I didn't."

"That sounds ominous. Besides, Judge Crowley made a big deal of showing her proper respect on the record. What's more, he—"

"Aleister's got a soft spot for the girl. So what?"

"He called her 'Your Grace,' and 'Her Royal Highness.'"

"Again, so what?"

"Well, who is she?" Sam sputtered.

Adam heaved a sigh. "I can't tell you that, Sam. Orders from on high."

"The Covenancy?"

Adam only looked at him, but he didn't deny it.

Sam whistled. "They usually don't get involved."

"And they did here. What's that tell you?" Adam turned and walked out of his office.

"That I'm going to have to be devious to find out what I want to know," Sam muttered.

22

Sam called Delilah Lara as his next witness, and as she was brought in from the holding cells, he couldn't help but stare up at Crowley. *He knows*, was all he could think. *He's a family friend... Who would Aleister Crowley befriend?*

As Lara was ushered to the witness box, she stared daggers at the fetch. Angie leaned close and whispered in his ear. "Her animosity could be a problem."

Sam nodded, but he didn't intend to do anything to curb Deli's temper. He wanted to see how the fetch would react—with a human's emotion or with a psychopomp's detachment.

"Mr. McCoy? Your witness," said Judge Crowley.

"Yes, Your Honor." Sam stood and forced his mind down the ordered avenues of procedure and his strategy for the case. "Ms. Lara, are you a succubus?"

Deli smiled and winked at the jury. "I am."

"And you work at a sex club called The Red Door in Times Square?"

"I did. Right now, I reside underground on Rikers Island." She lifted her arm and pointed at the defendant. *Because of her.*

"We'll get to that. For now, please confine yourself to answering the questions I ask."

She looked at him and quirked an eyebrow. "Are we playing truth or dare?" She waggled her brows suggestively.

"No, Ms. Lara, we are not. And, to avoid any further digressions, I'd like you to know I'm fully warded against your charms."

"Pity," muttered Deli. "It's been a while."

"Ms. Lara, I direct your attention to the defense table. Do you know the being sitting next to the magister for the defense?"

"I do."

"And from where do you know her?"

"She's the foul bitch that put a geas on me."

"Young lady! You will not speak that way in my courtroom!" snapped Judge Crowley.

"Aleister, Aleister, Aleister…" Deli shook her head. "I haven't been young for thousands of years—though you certainly were, and not so long ago."

"Mr. McCoy, you *will* control your witness, or I'll have her removed!"

Sam stepped closer to the witness box. "Cool it, Delilah," he murmured. "He controls your fate."

Deli inclined her head. "I'm sorry, Judge," she said. "I don't know what comes over me sometimes."

"See that it doesn't happen again."

She smirked at the jury. "Is it me, or has the temperature dropped a few degrees in here?"

One of the jurors sniggered. One of the *male* jurors.

Sam glanced at him, then glared at Deli as he moved to stand between her and the jury. "You said the defendant placed a geas on you. Do you know what its purpose was?"

"Yes. To do her dirty work. She didn't care that I knew. She told me no one would ever believe a slut over an ambassador."

"Hearsay, Your Honor," said Laveau, leaping to his feet.

"No, it isn't," said Crowley without looking at the magister for the defense. "Sit down, Mr. Laveau." He waved a languid hand at McCoy.

"Thank you, Your Honor," said Sam. "Ms. Lara, what was the compulsion the defendant placed on you? Please be as exact as you can."

"Would a direct quote help? I have hyperthymesia—I remember all of my experiences in vivid detail."

"If you can offer an exact quote, that would be fine."

"She said, 'When you see this boy—' and here she gave me his picture." Delilah went on in a voice that mimicked the fetch's. "'When you see this boy, you will seduce him using all of your wiles. You are to ensure he asks you for your services outside the club. Then, in the moment of his climax, end his existence on this plane as only your kind can. You will tell no one of this geas—not that anyone would believe a slut over an ambassador in any case.'"

"And what did you do in response?"

Delilah shrugged one pale, perfect shoulder that had slipped free from the neck of her blouse. "I did what she told me to."

"You took the victim's life?"

"I did. It has sustained me all these weeks."

Sam scoffed and shook his head. "No more questions, Your Honor."

"Very well, Mr. McCoy. Mr. Laveau? Have you questions for this witness?"

"You betcha, Judge."

"I beg your pardon, Mr. Laveau?"

"I mean to say: Yes, Your Honor. Thank you."

Crowley heaved a sigh and motioned him forward.

Laveau grinned at Delilah. "Hello, Ms. Lara. I must say you look quite fetching today."

"How very droll," said Deli.

"Maybe, but it illustrates my point, nonetheless. I noticed your little foreplay with the jury earlier. Were you attempting to seduce the jurors?"

"I believed they would be adequately warded. I just wanted to lighten the mood."

"Indeed," said Laveau, putting his hands behind his back and pacing toward the jury box. "But you did exercise your abilities?"

"I did."

"If you believed them to be warded, what was the point?"

Deli lifted that same pale shoulder and smiled at Laveau. "I like to test my abilities from time to time. I understand you do, too."

"Strike that last sentence, clerk," said Crowley. He turned to Delilah and glowered at her. "Ms. Lara, I want to caution you. You are not on trial *today*, but there can still be repercussions for your behavior here today. You'd do well to keep that in mind."

"Okay, Judge Crowley. I'll be good."

"See that you are."

Delilah turned her attention back to Laveau and tossed a wink his way.

He swallowed hard and cut his eyes away. "Uh, yes. Do you... Uh..." He cleared his throat and glared at his shoes, breathing long, slow breaths.

"Are you all right, Mr. Laveau?"

"Yes, Your Honor." He lifted his head and fixed Delilah Lara with a powerful stare. "Do you feel justified in drawing mundane lifeforce from unsuspecting mortals?"

"Yes," said Lara, then laughed at the gasps from the gallery.

"And why is that?"

"It is my right. My right as dictated by the Covenant of Improper Action." She turned her head to smile at the jury.

"You mean to say that consuming the lifeforce of mundanes is required for the maintenance of your life, as dictated by your nature?"

McCoy stood. "Your Honor, Ms. Lara is many things, but she is *not* a Covenant magister. She has no expertise with which to answer Mr. Laveau's question."

"Your Honor, I submit that she does. I'm not asking for her expert legal opinion on the Covenant, I'm asking for her *understanding* of it. Who could be a better expert on her understanding than Ms. Lara herself?"

"Indeed. Your objection is overruled, Mr. McCoy. The witness will answer."

"Yes, of course," said Lara. "I'm built by the Creator to drain lifeforce for sustenance. I've been gifted certain abilities in support of this by that same Creator."

"I see. Then, it is your belief that no murder has, in fact, occurred?"

"Not as judged by the Covenant of Improper Action."

"And you are here today because Mr. McCoy extorted your testimony by threatening you with a murder charge?"

"He charged me already," said Deli with yet another one-shouldered shrug.

"Your Honor!" snapped McCoy, coming up from his chair.

Crowley waved him back down. "No need to object, Mr. McCoy." He turned his baleful gaze on Laveau. "Let me explain a few salient points for you, Mr. Laveau. First, filing criminal charges against defendants cannot be characterized as extortion. Second, the witness is under no obligation to testify, or to continue testifying—though should she refuse to continue at this point, her testimony will be stricken *in toto*."

"It might not be extortion in the strictest sense, but—"

"No, Laveau. It is not extortion in *any* sense." Crowley pulsed and flashed his agitation at the courtroom. "Stop characterizing it as such

"Yes, Your Honor," said Laveau as he ducked his head.

"Now, if you have more questions, I suggest you move on with your cross."

"Yes, Your Honor." Laveau raised his head and treated them to a conspiratorial look. "Ms. Lara, are you testifying today as part of a plea agreement?"

"Yes."

"And what are the terms of the agreement as you understand them?"

"I'm to testify against the defendant, and in return, my charges will be reduced from various and sundry to simple killing without a license."

"And is there to be a sentence recommendation if you do a good job here today?"

"Mr. Laveau," growled Crowley. "I believe I've already spoken to this?"

"Sorry, Your Honor."

"Rephrase the question, or I will strike it."

Laveau nodded, a small smile on his lips. "What is to be your recommended sentence per your current charges and your plea bargain?"

"Well, the first charge is one lifetime. The second could be probation."

"Unlikely," muttered Crowley, though everyone in the courtroom heard him.

"I see. And one last question, Ms. Lara."

"Yes?"

"Would you be here today if you hadn't been charged with magical murder?"

"No."

Grinning at the jury, Laveau said, "Nothing further, Your Honor."

"Redirect, please, Your Honor," said Sam.

"Continue, Mr. McCoy."

"Ms. Lara," said Sam, standing and walking toward the jury box. He stopped and faced Delilah. "*Why* wouldn't you be here today if you hadn't been charged with magical murder?"

A slow grin spread across Lara's lips, and she winked at McCoy. "Because I'd still be under the effects of the defendant's geas."

"You'd still be compelled not to tell anyone. Is that correct?"

"Yes."

McCoy faced the jury. "And can you imagine why the defendant issued such a compulsion?"

"Objection, Your Honor."

"No, Mr. Laveau. I will allow this."

"Because she didn't want to be exposed. That's the whole reason she wanted me to eat the kid."

"Thank you, Ms. Lara." McCoy looked into the face of each juror, then, with that done, said, "Nothing further, Your Honor. The Prosecution rests."

23

Aleister Crowley hunched forward and looked down his nose at the defense table. "Mr. Laveau, are you ready to present your case?"

"Your Honor, I move that the prosecution has not proven their case, and I ask you to dismiss it with prejudice."

"You must be kidding," said Sam.

Judge Crowley held up a ghostly hand and made a placating tapping gesture at McCoy. "No, Mr. Laveau. Your motion is denied."

"Very well, Your Honor. In that case, I have a few witnesses?"

"Go ahead, Mr. Laveau."

"Yes, Your Honor. Thank you. For my first witness, I'd like to call Mr. McCoy."

"Your Honor!"

"You may not call the prosecutor, Mr. Laveau."

"But, Your Honor, Mr. McCoy is crucial to my case. He can testify as to his inappropriate arguments at the proceedings in the appellate court."

"Mr. Laveau," growled Crowley.

"Okay, fine, fine." Laveau trotted out his long-suffering, see-how-they're-all-against-me expression and waved it around. "In that case, I must call Judge Merlin of the Lexus Court of Appeals."

Crowley heaved a sigh and closed his eyes, giving every appearance of a frustrated father counting to ten before dealing with his child. "No, Mr. Laveau. Do you have *any* proper witnesses?"

Laveau's shoulders slumped, and he rolled his head forward. "Yes, Your Honor. I call Professor Anders Blight."

Crowley arched an eyebrow, then motioned the bailiff to fetch the witness. After he was sworn in, Crowley motioned for Laveau to proceed.

"Thank you, Judge. Professor Blight, a pleasure to see you again."

The professor was a white-haired, black-robed man with a stooped back. He wriggled to find a comfortable position in the witness box, then peered at Laveau. "Is that you, Geoffery?"

"Yes, Professor. It's Geoff Laveau, the magister for the defense in this trial."

"Ah, yes."

"Professor, can you tell the Court your position at the University of New York Locus?"

"Dean Emeritus of the Canonical School of Covenant Law."

"Thank you. Your Honor, I wish this witness to be certified as a Covenant expert witness."

"Any objection, Mr. McCoy?"

Sam waved his hands. "None, Your Honor."

"Very well. So ordered."

"Thank you, Judge Crowley," said Laveau. "Professor, what is your specific area of interest concerning the Covenant?"

"I have studied the Covenant of Improper Action for over one hundred years."

"And could you please explain to the court what the Covenant dictates?"

"Yes, of course. The Covenant of Improper Action simply states that any supernatural must be allowed to act as their nature dictates. Vampires must drink blood to survive, so blood-drinking charges may not be brought against them in criminal court. Witches and warlocks control magic fields, thus may not be prosecuted for doing so. Et cetera."

"And in your expert opinion, does the Covenant of Improper Action have a bearing on the case before the Court?"

"Most certainly."

McCoy drew his lips in a thin, straight line and suppressed a sigh.

"Can you please explain?"

"The defendant is a fetch. Her nature demands that she assume the identity of mortals so she may dispatch her duties as a psychopomp."

"I see. So, were a fetch to assume the identity of a human being, then act to protect that identity, she would be acting within the scope of the Covenant of Improper Action?"

"In my opinion, yes."

Laveau turned to McCoy with a self-satisfied smile. "Your witness."

McCoy leaned forward on his elbows. "Professor, are you aware of the recent ruling in the appellate court with regard to the defendant?"

"I am."

"And you're aware that five of the best legal minds have opined the defendant's actions are *not* protected under the Covenant?"

Professor Blight spread his hands and smiled. "Even the courts can make mistakes, Mr. McCoy."

McCoy ducked his chin to his chest, his face scrunched with concentration. "Professor, by the interpretation you've just provided, is there any crime a fetch may commit?"

"Well, of course. Any improper action that is not prescribed by her nature."

"But you've said that she can do anything to protect her assumed identity."

"Yes, that she may carry out her role as a psychopomp."

McCoy smiled. "And can you explain to the Court how serving as Ambassador to the United Nations is a prerequisite for a psychopomp?"

Blight frowned and tugged his long beard. "I can think of no reason."

McCoy got up and stepped around the table, his eyes on the jury. "Ah, I see. To clarify your position, then, if the defendant had killed to maintain her identity so she could get close to one who was about to pass from this life, that wouldn't be a crime, but if she killed for *any other reason*, it would be?"

"Yes, that seems proper."

"And you can think of no reason why the defendant would need to hold the ambassadorship and live in the Locus of New York?"

"No."

"Thank you, Professor Blight. It's been most educational." McCoy looked at Crowley and nodded. "That's all for me, Judge." He turned and smirked at Laveau. "Good try," he mouthed as he returned to his seat.

"Mr. Laveau? Anything else?"

Laveau sat very still. "Your Honor, may it please the Court, I'd like to ask for a continuance."

"To what end?"

Laveau shook his head and slumped. "I need time to review my position, Your Honor."

"Am I to take it that you have no more witnesses, then?"

Laveau closed his eyes.

"In the future, I'd counsel you not to put all your eggs in one basket. Is there no one else you can call on your client's behalf?"

"Your Honor, I do not know."

"Very well. I'll give you the balance of the day to see if you can come up with anything, Mr. Laveau. *But* if you cannot, you will rest your case and be prepared with your closing statement first thing tomorrow." Crowley focused on the gavel for a moment, then grasped it and issued a quick bang with it. "This Court stands in recess until nine tomorrow morning."

24

As Sam and Angie descended the Courthouse steps, Laveau scrambled down to meet them. "Mr. McCoy, can we talk?"

"To what end, Mr. Laveau?"

"I'd like to discuss a plea."

Sam shook his head and grinned at Angie. "You must be joking."

"Not at all. I'm trying to do my best by my client."

"Your best would have been to build a salient case that didn't depend only on one old man."

Laveau grimaced, then ducked his head. "Don't punish my client for my failures."

"Laveau, your client is charged with conspiracy to commit magical murder, psychic assault, and obstruction of justice. That is why she will be punished, and for no other reason." He turned to go, but then shifted his attention back to Laveau. "If I were you, Laveau, I'd focus on preparing to defend your actions in this case for the Magisterial Board of Ethical Conduct. You've already lost *this* case."

Sam and Angie left him standing dejected in the middle of the Courthouse steps.

25

The next morning at nine, Crowley called the court to order, then looked at Laveau. "Well?"

"Your Honor, the Defense rests."

Crowley gazed down at the man for a moment, his face darkening with a stern, solemn expression. "Mr. Laveau, be in my chambers ten minutes after the conclusion of this case."

"Yes, Your Honor," said a very pale Geoffrey Laveau.

"Are you prepared, at least, to offer *any* form of a closing?"

Laveau nodded.

"And you, Mr. McCoy? Are you prepared to carry on?"

"Yes, Your Honor."

"Then do so."

Sam stood and walked to the jury box. He rested his hands on the railing that separated them from the rest of the court. After looking them each in the eye, he began.

"Ladies and gentlemen of the jury, take a look at the defendant sitting there by Mr. Laveau. She appears harmless—just another woman living her life. But, she's nothing of the sort. We can't even say for certain she is indeed female.

"We can say, however, that she's committed conspiracy to commit magical murder. She compelled the murder of Edward Thompson by means of a geas and is as responsible as though she'd drained his lifeforce herself. Yes, Delilah Lara is a succubus, and yes, Ms. Lara committed the actual act. But"—he held up his index finger—"Ms. Lara was acting under the power of the defendant's magical compulsion.

"This leads us to the charge of psychic assault. The defendant not only compelled the actions of Ms. Lara but also of two police detectives, their lieutenant, an Assistant Locus Magister—my assistant, Ms. Carmichael, whom you've seen sitting beside me every day of this trial—and...*and* the defendant placed her geas on me.

"As heinous as I find the act on a personal level, I'd like you to consider the broader picture as well. I am the Executive Assistant Locus Magister. My role is second only to the LM, himself. Ms. Carmichael works on a variety of cases for the LM's office and is an officer of the court. The two detectives and their lieutenant are part of our first line of defense against the chaos that would surely follow if we abandoned the Canon and Covenants. A psychic attack on the five of us is tantamount to a subversion of the entire legal process—to wit, obstruction of justice.

"The magister for the defense will get up in a moment and argue that the fetch known as Jane Doe committed all these acts because it is her nature to do so. It might surprise you to hear, but I agree with him." Sam turned and gazed evenly at the stunned Laveau, then turned back to the jury. "But it is *not* the nature of her race. Her actions are not shielded by the Covenant of Improper Action because, simply put, Jane Doe did not act following the nature of her race. She is not here to act as a psychopomp, but rather to further her own mysterious agenda.

"For these reasons, you must find the defendant guilty on all counts. There is no wiggle room, not in accordance with the Canon and Covenants we all live by." Sam inclined his head. "Thank you for your patience and attention. I'm sure you'll do the right thing."

He returned to his seat, studiously not looking at Laveau, who climbed slowly to his feet and plodded toward the jury box.

"Ladies and gentlemen, my colleague, Mr. McCoy, speaks eloquently about the Covenants, about justice, and about the law. I'm sure you'll agree that he's a fine magister, and that he fulfills his role in the Locus Magister's office admirably.

"On the other hand, I'm sure we can also agree that I'm not in his league. I don't have his experience before the Bar, as a litigator, nor do I have his expert use of language. But I do have his passion.

"This is not a case of black and whites, as Mr. McCoy would have you believe. My client is admittedly a fetch—a being whose sole purpose on this plane is to assume the identity of others and live out the rest of their lives.

"Now, Mr. McCoy argues that the Covenant of Improper Action is inapplicable to my client's defense, using the technical argument that the purpose of her life is to act as a psychopomp. But, ladies and gentlemen, when was the last time you heard anyone speak of a psychopomp outside of academic discussions?

"When is the last time you've seen one acting in his role?" He scoffed. "When is the last time you've *seen* one outside of this courtroom?

"Who among you has seen Anubis? Or Yama? Charon? A Valkyrie?" He held up his hands and grinned. "Oh, I know. Ancient history, right?

"Fine. What about Shiva assuming the aspect of Tarakeshwara? A Visnuduta? A Yamaduta? Daena? Azrael?

"I've never seen any of these beings acting in their role as a psychopomp. Before this case, I'd never wondered about it, never considered why they no longer assumed their mantles as escorts from this world to the next." He favored them with a winning smile. "I bet you hadn't either. And there's a reason behind it all.

"That reason is that our culture no longer requires such beings. Even the religions of the mundane make virtually no mention of psychopomps. No, the role of these entities fades out, day by day, and quite soon will no longer exist.

"What, then, is my client to do? Should she simply stop being a fetch? Might as well ask His Honor to stop being a ghost, or a wraith to stop influencing the minds and lives of their hosts.

"Should my client stop assuming identities when she does not have one of her own?" A mantle of sadness fell over him. "Can we ask her to simply give up and fade out of existence because her role is no longer explicitly necessary?

"I tell you no. We have no right to ask this of her.

"What, then, is her *new* nature? What governs what is applicable under the Covenant of Improper Action? What is her *nature* now?" Laveau stepped to the jury box rail and leaned over it. "If you think it's just to ask her to fade from the world, vote her guilty, but if you find that as distasteful as I do, then you must acquit her." He dropped his gaze to the floor. "I wish to thank you, ladies and gentlemen, as well as the Court, for putting up with my failures and inexperience. Please don't punish my client for my failings."

"Your Honor, I must object. I move that Mr. Laveau's entire closing be stricken from the record, and ask that the jury is instructed to disregard it."

Laveau looked at the jury through eyes filled with sadness and a small, tortured smile on his lips.

Judge Crowley scowled down at McCoy. "It's his closing statement, sir. He's allowed to present any argument he wishes."

"But, Your Honor! He's asking them to nullify!"

Crowley leaned back, his substance flickering. "No, I don't think so, Mr. McCoy. His questions are hard to answer, and I'll let the jury consider them."

McCoy sat down with a grimace.

Angie leaned close. "I've been watching the jury. We might be in trouble—jurors five, nine, and twelve are almost in tears."

"Do you wish to rebut?"

Sam thought for a moment, then shook his head. "No, Your Honor. I've said everything I have to say on the matter."

"Very well. Ladies and gentlemen of the jury, we've reached the end of the formal presentation of the cases. You've heard the evidence, the opinions, and the arguments from both the prosecution and the defense. It now falls to you to render a verdict. I must admonish you to follow the Canon and Covenants *as they are now written*. You may not consider 'what should be.' I charge you to do your duties under the law, to consider the facts of the case, and return with a verdict of guilty or non-guilty on each of the charges in exclusion of the others. If you have questions of record, the clerk will provide you with transcripts. If you wish to examine a piece of evidence, Bailiff Haddo will bring it. If you have questions as to the law, you may send a message to me, and I will answer it." He gazed at them solemnly. "Are there any questions?"

There weren't, and he gaveled the court
adjourned.

CHAPTER 4

THE VERDICT

I

Angie stuck her head through Sam's door. "Adam wants to see us." Without waiting, she turned and crossed the hall.

Sam sighed and got to his feet. He followed Angie into Adam's office and slumped onto the couch.

Adam favored him with a crooked smile. "The cases that seem easy sometimes turn out to be the hardest."

Sam nodded.

"Mr. Laveau's closing hurt us."

"It did," said Sam.

"How bad?"

Sam sighed and grimaced, shaking his head.

"Three of the jurors became teary-eyed. I think we might be in trouble," said Angie.

"Offer Laveau a deal."

"We can't do that, Adam," said Sam, eyes blazing. "It would be a miscarriage of justice!"

"What we can't do is allow the jury to nullify the verdict. It happens in mundane courts, but not in ours. Make a deal and put the fetch in a dungeon. Some time is better than no time at all."

"I won't do it," said Sam. "It's my—"

"*You serve at my pleasure, Sam!*" snapped Adam, his voice thundering and crackling with power.

Sam shook his head, looking sad.

"Make Laveau an offer before the jury comes back and lets this fetch walk out of court a free...whatever it is."

Sam scoffed and left the office, waving his hand at Angie.

"I'll set up a meeting," she said.

2

Sam sat behind his desk, chair swiveled to show the room his back. Laveau and his client sat at the table placed perpendicular to his desk. Angie sat across from them.

"But why?" asked Laveau. "You didn't seem interested before the closing arguments."

"Call it an act of mercy," said Angie.

Laveau shook his head, a predatory grin blooming on his face. "No, I don't think that's it. I think my closing scared you."

Sam whirled his chair around, eyes blazing. "Your closing is tantamount to asking the jury to nullify. Don't you understand the precedent you've unwittingly put into play? Don't you get it, Laveau?"

"Who said I did it unwittingly?" His grin widened into a self-satisfied smile. "But, okay. Point taken. We'll consider your offer as long as it has no time attached."

Sam stared at him for a moment in stunned disbelief. "Don't misconstrue your position, Laveau."

"Probation, then."

"You're kidding."

But he wasn't, and Sam smiled at his back as he left. "Adam couldn't possibly have meant for us to let her off completely," he said to Angie.

3

Adam entered Sam's office without knocking, swinging the door wide and letting it bang against the wall. "I told you to make a deal."

"Laveau wouldn't go for a deal."

"*Make* him."

"Adam, he won't accept anything but no jail time. I'm not willing to do that."

Adam narrowed his eyes and stood glowering at Sam for the space of a couple of angry breaths. "*You're* not willing to do that. You'd better hope the *jury* isn't willing to do that, too."

"They won't. They will see through Laveau's tactics."

"They will? Since when did you become an expert on what juries will do?" Without waiting for an answer, Adam turned and left the office, slamming the door behind him.

Sam stared after him, a wry grin twisting his features.

4

An hour later, the jury signaled that they had a verdict. Sam and Angie rushed back to the courthouse, and truth be told, neither of them felt as confident as they appeared. In the hall, they passed Oriscoe and Nogan, who loitered near a window. The detectives gave them a thumbs-up and broad smiles.

After they'd made it to the prosecution table and arranged themselves, Bailiff Haddo bade them all rise. Crowley came floating in without bothering with anything as silly as opening the door and assumed the bench. After calling the court in session, he turned to the jury. "Madam Foreperson, I understand you have a verdict?"

A lanky woman with lupine features stood and nodded. "We do, Your Honor."

Crowley held out an ethereal hand, and Haddo ferried the folded verdict form from the foreperson to the judge. The judge struggled in his attempt to grab an edge for a moment, then shook the paper open. He read it and nodded down at the foreperson. "Please deliver the verdict." He allowed Haddo to take the document and return it to the jury.

The foreperson turned slightly to face more of the courtroom, her eyes resting on the defendant.

"On the first count of the indictment, conspiracy to commit magical murder in the first degree, how do you find?" asked Crowley.

"We find the defendant guilty as charged, Your Honor."

"And the second of psychic assault in the first degree?"

"Guilty, Your Honor."

Crowley tilted his head back and glanced at the defendant. "And the final count of obstruction of justice in the first degree?"

"Guilty, Your Honor."

"Very well, Madam Foreperson. Was this a unanimous verdict?"

"Yes, Your Honor."

"For all counts?"

"Yes, Your Honor."

Crowley nodded, smiling down at her. "The Court thanks you for your service. The jury is dismissed. Sentencing will occur tomorrow at two. Bailiff, take the prisoner away. Court is dismissed."

As Sam turned, he spotted Adam standing in the back of the gallery. Adam smiled and tipped him a wink.

CHAPTER 5

THE AFTERMATH

I

The fetch was sentenced to a lifetime and a half and shipped off to Attica within the week. Delilah Lara drew a reduced sentence of five years' probation, which meant she'd need to find alternate employment, but she seemed content with that.

As Sam left Judge Crowley's courtroom, he spotted Oriscoe striding down the hall toward him with a crooked smile and a twinkle in his eye. "Nice going, Counselor."

"Thanks. You, too, Detective. Your insight about the fetch saved us a lot of headaches."

"Aw, shucks," said Leery.

"Next time, try not to get yourself geased."

Leery chuckled. "You, too, McCoy." After a nod at McCoy, he lifted his chin as if sniffing the wind and stepped around him. He strode off down the hall, a bounce in his step, flipping his scarf around his neck, then belting his camel hair coat tighter around his middle.

As Leery pushed out into the cold, Angie stepped from the courtroom, already wearing her coat, scarf, and fetching sable hat. "What's he so happy about?" she asked after glancing at Leery's retreating back.

"My guess is, he's got a date."

"A date?"

McCoy glanced at her and wagged his eyebrows.

"With Deli?" Angie scoffed, then glanced at the closing door. "You've got to be *kidding*."

"Never underestimate a wolf's libido."

Angie cocked an eyebrow at Sam, then shook her head.

McCoy shrugged. "I could be wrong. Did you do what I asked?"

Angie's lips flattened into a grim line. "I did, but I didn't like doing it."

"I know. What did you find out from your Covenancy friend?"

"Her mother's the Witch Queen."

"Oh, *that* Drusilla." Sam treated her to a half shake of his head. "That changes things a bit, don't you think?"

Angie shrugged and tilted her head to the side. "Not until it does. Do you know how many witches revere her mother as a goddess?"

"I do. She will bear watching."

Angie shook her head. "Not by me, and not by my friend in the Covenancy. Verbius made that quite clear."

"You can't tell me you don't have a problem with the potential bias."

"She hasn't shown a hint of anything of the sort so far. In fact, from what Deli told me, her bias goes the other way, if it exists at all." Angie shook her head once more. "We owe her the benefit of the doubt."

"Do we?" Sam mused.

Angie squinted at him for a moment.

"Do you worship Agrat bat Mahlat?" Sam asked her.

"That's none of your business, Sam." She turned and began walking toward the door. After a few steps, she stopped and turned. "Do you think Oriscoe knows?"

"That old wolf? I'd be surprised if he couldn't smell it."

With a nod and wave, Angie turned and walked out into the cold. After a few moments of silent contemplation of the floor tiles, Sam followed her.

I hope you've enjoyed this introduction to the CLAW & WARDER world and can't wait for the next episode. You can find the next episode, *Arms Dealers: CLAW & WARDER Episode 2,* here: https://ehv4.us/4cw2.

If you've enjoyed this novel, please consider joining my Readers Group by visiting https://ehv4.us/join. Or follow me on BookBub by visiting my profile page there: https://ehv4.us/bbub.

For my complete bibliography, please visit: https://ehv4.us/bib.

Books these days succeed or fail based on the strength of their reviews. I hope you will consider leaving a review—as an independent author, I could use your help. It's easy (I promise). Complete instructions for leaving your review can be found below.

To leave a review, please:

1. Visit: https://ehv4.us/2revcw1
2. Sign-in if prompted
3. Select your star rating

4. Write a few short words (or a lot of long words, whatever you are comfortable with)
5. Click the submit button
6. Accept my sincere gratitude

AUTHOR'S NOTE

This book is dedicated to Jerry Orbach, also known as Lenny Briscoe to fans of Law & Order. He was my favorite character, and I was sad to see him go. His sense of humor, his one-liners, his gallows humor, is what made this book so attractive to me. I didn't know the man, but I have a feeling he would enjoy the idea of a combination of Lenny Briscoe and a Hassidic werewolf sharing the same skin—just think of all the jokes that fall out of that pairing.

I had a blast writing this story—not only was the work itself a lot of fun, but it gave me a great excuse to laugh and carry on with one of my closest friends, Stephen Jacobs, over bacon cheeseburgers in our favorite lunch spot. Steve is a guy everyone likes—not only funny and willing to laugh at almost everything but also compassionate and caring—and I'm both lucky and blessed to have him as my friend.

I also want to thank those members of my Readers' Group who have kindly allowed me to use their names in this book: Delilah Lara, Edward Thompson, Fiona Rae Gill, Kylelynn Fubelli, and Amie Brewer. I had a good time making your namesakes jump through hoops. It's purely coincidence that the two Irish characters are Irish in real life.

No, really.

ABOUT THE AUTHOR

Erik Henry Vick is an author who happens to be disabled by an autoimmune disease (also known as his Personal Monster™). He writes to hang on to the few remaining shreds of his sanity. His current favorite genres to write are dark fantasy and horror.

He lives in Western New York with his wife, Supergirl; their son; a Rottweiler named after a god of thunder; and two extremely psychotic cats. He fights his Personal Monster™ daily with humor, pain medicine, and funny T-shirts.

Erik has a B.A. in Psychology, an M.S.C.S., and a Ph.D. in Artificial Intelligence. He has worked as a criminal investigator for a state agency, a college professor, a C.T.O. for an international software company, and a video game developer.

He'd love to hear from you on social media:

Blog: https://erikhenryvick.com
Twitter: https://twitter.com/BerserkErik
Facebook: https://fb.me/erikhenryvick
Amazon author pages:
    USA: https://ehv4.us/amausa
    UK: https://ehv4.us/amauk
Goodreads Author Page: https://ehv4.us/gr
BookBub Author Profile: http://ehv4.us/bbub

Made in the USA
Coppell, TX
23 July 2020